"When you're born into the Devereaux family, your place is pretty much decided from conception. Long story short, in my grandfather's eyes, I don't measure up."

She tapped her fingers against her thigh, a move he was sure she did absentmindedly. But to him, it just brought back the memory of how good those elegant fingers felt against his naked flesh.

*Focus, Lennox.*

"Why doesn't your grandfather recognize your worth? Do you have a habit of making bad deals?"

She shook her head. "No. I know what I want, and I have no qualms about reaching beyond the limits others have placed on me. But to my grandfather, that looks like impulsive recklessness. If I were a man, he'd call me a trailblazer."

She leaned forward, placing a warm hand on top of his. "I'm sorry for putting you in a compromising position. It was never my intention. And if you want to call the whole deal off, I'll accept that. I just need to know where you want to go from here."

"Well, in my mind, how we proceed depends on how you answer my next question."

She narrowed her gaze as she leaned forward. "What's that?"

"Are you carrying my child?"

* * *

*One Night Expectations* by LaQuette
is part of the Devereaux Inc. series.

Dear Reader,

Here's another Devereaux Inc. story featuring scandal, family drama and sizzling attraction in Brooklyn's historic Clinton Hill.

In *One Night Expectations*, ambitious Amara Devereaux-Rodriguez is livid when she doesn't get the promotion she deserves. To spite the grandfather standing in her way of ascension, she conceals her identity and spends one sinful night with Lennox Carlisle in all his sexy, powerful glory. Although their passion blazes hot enough to pop a fire hydrant, Amara knows she can never have more than one night. Her career must come first. Even if it means sacrificing her need for Lennox, she'll do it just to accomplish her goal.

Lennox is trying to relax before the last leg of his campaign begins when the sexy brown-skinned angel in the stiletto pumps snatches his attention. Overwhelmed by passion, he gives in to his desire for her. Although furious when he discovers Amara's identity, he still can't walk away. First, every time he's in the same room with her, he wants to consume her. Second, she's carrying his child. If news of her pregnancy gets out, their complicated entanglement will ruin Lennox's chance to win the election. Determined to have his child and win the race, there's only one solution to his problem. Amara has to marry him, and if she won't agree, he'll destroy Devereaux Inc. and the position she's longed for without the slightest hesitation to force her down the aisle.

Keep it sexy!

*LaQuette*

# LAQUETTE

## ONE NIGHT EXPECTATIONS

Recycling programs
for this product may
not exist in your area.

ISBN-13: 978-1-335-73561-4

One Night Expectations

For questions and comments about the quality of this book,
please contact us at CustomerService@Harlequin.com.

Harlequin Enterprises ULC
22 Adelaide St. West, 41st Floor
Toronto, Ontario M5H 4E3, Canada
www.Harlequin.com

Printed in U.S.A.

DEIA activist **LaQuette** writes bold stories featuring multicultural characters. Her writing style brings intellect to the drama. She crafts emotionally epic tales that are deeply pigmented by reality's paintbrush. This Brooklyn native's novels are a unique mix of unapologetically sexy, stylish and sensational characters who are confident in their right to appear on the page.

### Books by LaQuette

#### *Devereaux Inc.*

*A Very Intimate Takeover*
*Backstage Benefits*
*One Night Expectations*

Visit the Author Profile page at Harlequin.com, or www.laquette.com, for more titles.

You can also find LaQuette on Facebook, along with other Harlequin Desire authors, at www.Facebook.com/harlequindesireauthors!

To my ride or die and fellow Brooklynite,
my agent, Latoya Smith.
Thank you for helping me show the world
what two little brown girls from Brooklyn can do.

# One

"I said what I said."

Amara Angel Devereaux-Rodriguez sat at her desk on a Zoom call with her grandfather, internally reeling from the five words he'd just spoken. His tone was casual, as if he was sitting at home with his feet up reading a newspaper, not discussing contracts totaling more than a quarter of a small country's GDP.

But that was what made her grandfather so good at what he did. He was so unassuming, he was deadly. By the time opposing counsel figured this out, he'd already have the deal signed, sealed and delivered.

"You can't do this, Granddaddy." Her voice was calm but her clenched teeth and stiff body language accurately relayed her displeasure. "I've put in too much work for this company for you to pull the rug out from under me like this."

He was unmoved as he sat in the den at Devereaux Manor, dipping his gaze to read the document he was holding. Only when he was finished did he pull off his readers and look up, finally acknowledging her presence on the video call.

"Can't?" He raised a brow as he sat up straight in his chair. "As lead counsel for Devereaux Inc. and your boss, I can do whatever I want. Just because I'm out of the office spending time with your uncle Ace while he's sick doesn't mean I'm not still in charge. My decision is final. I'm not retiring until after this Falcon Development deal is closed."

She folded her arms, trying her best to suppress the anger boiling inside. "I have closed more deals and made more money for this company in the last three years than any other lawyer here, including you. You were poised to sail off into the sunset and give me the reins. Then all of a sudden you're changing your plans and pushing me to the sidelines. What the hell, Granddaddy?"

She realized two seconds after she'd said it her mouth had written a check her ass couldn't cash. David Devereaux might've been her sweet grandfather, but he didn't tolerate disrespect from anyone. And by the way he was slowly leaning into the screen, she realized shit was about to get very real.

"That right there is the reason I'm not handing the reins over to you yet. You're brilliant and determined. But you don't know how to get what you want without bulldozing your way through every problem."

"My methods have never been a problem before, certainly not when I was making this company more money than it could count. I fail to see the problem now."

"The problem…" He paused and stared into the screen. She could tell the moment his features softened and his shoulders relaxed that he'd gone from seeing her as an insubordinate employee to his only grandbaby.

He calmly leaned back in his chair, folding his long arms across his chest. He was tall and lean, wearing the navy blue Brooks Brother suit he adored. Even though he was working from her uncle's home, the power suit dominated any corporate space he was in, whether it was the office or on the computer screen.

The same kind, dark brown eyes that had always shone with pride in Amara were tinged with sadness that moved something in her, even though she tried hard to ignore it.

"The problem," he continued, "is that your all-or-nothing approach doesn't work for some deals. Your greatest strength and weakness is that you always go in for the best financial deal. Money is great, but it ain't everything, baby girl. And the fact that you don't know that yet troubles me. It's gonna land you in a world of trouble. Success comes from the heart, not the bank account. And because you don't understand that, you let Falcon stipulate that we're responsible for securing the building permits from the city council in exchange for a better financial return for Devereaux Inc."

She shrugged. He was always going on about heart. Heart didn't pay the bills, though. Only cold, hard cash did that.

"I fail to see the problem. We're getting more money in exchange for dealing with the permits ourselves. It's bureaucracy. We have experience cutting through red tape. What's the issue?"

He shook his head as he looked up to the ceiling like he was asking for celestial grace to deal with her.

"You're right. Bureaucracy usually wouldn't pose a problem for us. But the particular area where we're building is smack-dab in the middle of Lennox Carlisle's district. If you'd bothered to learn anything about the councilman, you'd know he blames companies like ours for gentrification and running residents out of this neighborhood. And now he's running for mayor on the same issues. That's why Falcon made it a contractual obligation for us to get the permits instead of them. Carlisle has been slapping Falcon down every chance he gets. Now we can expect similar treatment. But your zeal to secure the bag blinded you to that. So here we are."

Amara flinched as if he'd struck her. Sure, this city councilman hadn't factored into her thinking when she inked the deal. But she was meticulous when it came to wheeling and dealing. If this bureaucrat was so problematic, she would've known about it.

"This isn't a big issue, Granddaddy. It's a minor detail."

"The fact that you don't see this as a problem is why I can't have you leading this deal. Carlisle can't be swayed by the trappings of wealth like other politicians. And since your focus is always money, he'll never give us what we need if you take the lead on these negotiations. He needs heart, Amara, and you don't speak his language. My decision is final. I want you nowhere near this deal."

"You'd never do this to my mother. If she were still practicing here—"

"If she were still practicing here," he interrupted, "I wouldn't have to tell her this. She'd know it already. Your mother retiring from practicing law was the worst hit this company has ever taken. If she and your father weren't so happy traipsing around Brooklyn so carefree, I'd still beg her to return. She understood that you need both heart and skill to win. I'm still waiting for you to learn that lesson."

She thought to defend herself for a hot second, until she saw disappointment cloud his eyes. Nothing she said would matter. Especially not when he was yet again comparing her to her mother. No one could reach the pedestal Ja'Net Devereaux-Rodriguez had been perched on since she graduated law school decades ago. Least of all Amara, the daughter who had her brains, but not her grace.

"I don't have time for this. I have to call Jeremiah and get him down to the office. Martha's up to something and whatever it is, it can't be good. We have to be prepared if she tries to disrupt the vote to appoint Trey CEO today."

Amara wasn't just using a diversion tactic, either. The company her great-uncle Ace Devereaux had turned into a billion-dollar enterprise was in crisis now that he was ill. His fiercest protector, Jeremiah Benton, whom Ace had taken in as his ward when Jeremiah was sixteen, had been leading the business, trying to keep Ace's sister, Martha, from staging a boardroom coup and destroying everything he'd built. And now Jeremiah had a new ally in Trey Devereaux, Ace's granddaughter who'd recently rejoined the fold after years of estrangement. Trey was up for appointment as CEO in accordance with Ace's rules of succession. Which ruffled Martha's feathers, to put it mildly, since she thought she was owed the job.

Amara inhaled slowly before getting in the last word with her grandfather. "You'll regret this." Her voice was full of calm and control, as befitted her upbringing. But before he could respond, she ended the call.

She wouldn't allow him to raise her blood pressure over this. Devereauxs didn't get mad. They got even. She just had to figure out what that looked like in this situation.

"If all you're going to do is stand there staring at me and not help me to stop Jeremiah and Trey from stealing this company, you can scatter like the rest of the scared little roaches that just left this room."

Amara stood in the mostly empty conference room staring at her great-aunt Martha. The impromptu board meeting that Amara had worried so much about had taken place a few moments ago with pleasing results. Well, pleasing for the company and those trying to save it. Not so much for Martha after the board had voted Trey and Jeremiah in as co-CEOs.

"Aunt Martha," Amara began carefully, "I know today's events were…disappointing for you. But I think if you took the time to get to know Trey, you'd feel a lot more confident with her and Jeremiah running the company. I know you can't see it now. But this is best for Devereaux Inc., for the family."

Martha stood up slowly, splaying her fingers flat on the large conference room table. "Best for the family?" Her voice was eerily calm, making the hairs on Amara's neck stand on end. "Sweet Amara. You most of all should understand that what's good for the business and family never seems to be good for the women doing all the work."

"What are you talking about, Auntie? Trey is a woman in this family."

"Trey is a puppet being used to keep my brother's antiquated succession rule in place long after he's dead and gone. Those of us who would breathe life into the company, take it in a new direction, are always sidelined."

Amara tried to make sense of Martha's words. "Auntie, it's been a long few days dealing with Ace's unexpected hospitalization and now this. My brain is too tired to piece together the meaning of your riddles."

Martha's smile sent a cold chill down Amara's back. The older woman casually grabbed her clutch and placed it under her arm.

"Amara, you're smart, determined, and you buck against every rule my brothers have established for how this business is run. You more than anyone should understand what I'm talking about. Everything you've ever wanted has been denied you because you don't do things the way your grandfather wants, while he praises your mother, a woman who did everything exactly according to his rules."

She stepped closer to Amara, placing a hand softly

against her cheek and offering her a soft, sincere smile that shook Amara to her core.

"Do you enjoy being treated as an afterthought in the family? Do you feel content to live in the shadow of you mother's accomplishments?"

Amara didn't answer, partly because Martha's questions were rhetorical. But mostly because she feared what her answer would actually be.

"Grandniece, if you don't fight for what you're owed," Martha warned, "you'll find yourself in the same place as me, villainized, rejected and forgotten by those who are supposed to love you."

"Aunt Martha," Amara interrupted. "I'm not you."

"You're the me of your generation, grandniece. And if you're not careful, you'll end up dedicating years of your life to this family and to this company with nothing to show for it."

"I think you're exaggerating a bit, Auntie."

Martha lifted a brow, giving Amara that "young'un, you don't know what you're talking about" look.

Silent, Martha placed a gentle kiss on Amara's cheek and exited, leaving her there to comb through everything the woman had said.

She didn't want to admit it, but Amara saw the parallels between Martha and herself. The worst part however wasn't admitting Martha was right. The worst thing was the fear that her pain might one day make her just as bitter and resentful as her great-aunt.

"Amaretto sour, Ian, and your best bag of pretzels." The friendly bartender at The Vault threw Amara a nod as she secured her phone inside her assigned locker and headed for the empty stool at the end of the bar.

If you were wealthy with any hint of celebrity, a membership at The Vault meant you could have a drink or five and not worry about it ending up in the tabloids. Electronic devices were prohibited, and the Brooklyn VIPs and power players entering the premises had to relinquish their phones in order to gain entry and be served.

"Rough day?"

Rough didn't begin to describe it. "If you call losing the promotion you were primed for because your boss sees you as too aggressive to get the job done right, yeah, it's been a rough day."

"Damn, someone at work actually played the aggressive Black woman card with you?" He shook his head. "Sounds like you deserve a double, then." He poured a healthy dose of the cocktail in her tumbler and slid it to her with a large bowl of pretzels. "Let me know if you need a refill on either."

"Definitely a refill on the drink. An order of hot wings would be great, too."

He gave her a thumbs-up and put her order in.

Relieved to have a moment of solitude, she looked at her drink and the bowl of pretzels and sighed. How cliché was her existence that she was sulking about the developments at work, nursing her wounds with alcohol and carbs at a bar. But Ian was right. Her grandfather had played the aggressive Black woman card and the more she thought about it, the more it pissed her off.

Being born to an African American mother and an Afro-Cuban father, she'd long ago learned how Black women were stereotyped. What was throwing her here was that it was coming from her own family.

Amara had never wanted to work anywhere else but Devereaux Inc. Why would she? It was a "for us by us" situation where she didn't have to navigate the misogynoir present in many corporate spaces. She could display her brilliance and excel without having to deal with bullshit. Except her grandfather's refusal to step down and allow her to lead was another kind of foolishness altogether.

She was the best Devereaux Inc. had to offer, and it still wasn't good enough for her to get the promotion she deserved.

"How did I end up here?"

"Not sure." A smooth, deep voice pulled her attention away from the pity party of one she was trying to have. "But I can't say I'm necessarily mad you are."

There was a smart-assed retort on the tip of her tongue until she looked up and saw the face that went with the voice. The man had golden-brown skin, hazel eyes, and a thin, dark brown goatee framing thick, full lips. She was so busy soaking up his good looks she couldn't find the sour retort she'd usually have waiting for a weak line like that.

But there was something more than his good looks that captivated her. He was vaguely familiar.

He stretched out his hand as he offered her a wide, easy smile. "I'm Len."

When she didn't immediately respond, he dropped his hand while dipping his head in an apologetic nod.

"I'm sorry, I didn't mean to bother you. I'll leave you to your drink."

She looked into his eyes, and recognition hit her. This was Lennox Carlisle, the very person at the center of her work woes. She searched his eyes, waiting to see if he recognized her as well. But to her surprise he didn't seem to.

"It's fine," she responded. "I've just had a long day. I didn't mean to be rude."

"Wanting to be left alone with your own thoughts isn't rude. And just because I wanted to speak to you doesn't mean you're obligated to give me the time of day. I apologize for interrupting you."

He stood up, tapping the counter to get the bartender's attention. "Hey, Ian, anything she orders tonight is on me."

"That's not necessary."

He shrugged. "It's not. But everybody deserves a break here and there. Hope your day gets better."

He smiled once more then turned toward the long hallway that led to the restrooms and offices. She watched his retreating form, not exactly certain of what had just happened, but not exactly put off by it, either.

While her grandfather had proven himself to be a misogynistic jerk, this stranger had offered her a small measure of kindness that somehow sparked hope inside her. Hope for what? She had no clue.

But she was curious to find out.

# Two

"Hey man, where you at?"

Lennox looked up at the sound of Carter's voice. His best friend was sitting on the edge of the desk in the middle of the room.

"Sorry," Lennox answered. "My head was elsewhere."

"I know," Carter replied. "I told you, no work when you're within these walls. Stop worrying about your next debate and relax a little with your boy."

Lennox slid into a relaxed slouch on the small sofa, spreading his arms across the back.

"I wish it were work that has me so preoccupied." When his friend lifted a questioning brow, Lennox sighed, closing his eyes as he dropped his head back against the sofa cushions.

Carter and Lennox's friendship went as far back as junior high school in Bedford-Stuyvesant when Carter's Puerto Rican parents moved their family from the Bronx to Brooklyn. Besides blood, there wasn't anyone Lennox trusted more, which was why Carter Jimenez was the only person he could let his guard down around.

"Sorry, man. I ran into this woman at the bar…"

"Someone you know?"

Lennox shook his head. "I don't think I've ever seen her here before."

"Considering you haven't spent an enormous amount of time here since I opened three years ago, that's not so strange."

Lennox chuckled. "The low-key shade isn't necessary. It's not like you're at my office every other day."

Carter shrugged. "You're a politician. Who wants to hang out in your stuffy office with people who lie like they breathe? My place of business is the hottest spot for folks like you to chill without cameras flashing in your face. Everybody wants to come here."

He wasn't wrong. If Lennox could spend more time here than at his office, he'd definitely do it. But when you were trying to keep the little guy from getting squashed by big corporations, there wasn't a whole lot of time for chilling at your best friend's lounge.

"So, what's up with this woman? She one of your constituents?"

"No clue. Apparently, she was having a rough day."

Carter folded his arm as a devilish grin curled his lips. "Let me guess, she wouldn't happen to have been gorgeous." When Lennox didn't answer Carter let out a howl. "Man, stop acting like you're worried about this stranger's welfare. If you saw something you like, shoot your shot."

"Says the man who's been single for—" A cloud of sadness shrouded his friend's face and Lennox instantly regretted his careless tongue. "Man, I'm sorry. I didn't mean to—"

Carter ran his hands up and down his thighs, taking a deep breath before settling his gaze back on Lennox.

"Don't apologize, Len. You're right, I shouldn't be giving dating advice. Mich has been gone for four years and I still haven't found the nerve to start dating again. She was my world."

"You've had a lot to deal with, Carter. Losing Michelle in a tragic accident and having to raise a one-year-old by yourself, that'd be a lot for the strongest shoulders. The fact that you've been able to do that and start a successful business, it's more than I could've handled under the same circumstances. Speaking of my goddaughter, how's Nevaeh?"

Lennox thought of Carter's five-year-old daughter, who pretty much ran the man's life, and his too whenever he was around.

"I think she's been talking to my mother too much. Mommy was grilling me about working too hard and not having someone special. Ever since then, Nevaeh has been pointing out all the pretty men and women she thinks I should date."

Lennox shook his head and laughed. He could definitely see Nevaeh doing something like that. A few months ago Nevaeh had walked in on a conversation Carter and his mother were having about her friend's son who was bisexual and single. When they realized the girl was in the room, Carter didn't even blink. He simply sat her down and explained in very age-appropriate terms that he was attracted to both men and women.

That was the thing Lennox admired most about his friend. When it came to his daughter, his default was to do what needed to be done. That meant he never shied away from the hard or awkward parts of being a parent.

"Mrs. Jimenez is a mess. Remind me to stay away from her before she starts in on my nonexistent love life."

"Well, considering you've been sitting in my office for the last half hour thinking about someone you saw at my bar, I'd say she has less to worry about when it comes to your love life than mine."

Lennox waved a dismissive hand. "Nah, man. My campaign is in full swing. Now is not the time for me to get involved with someone."

"Who said anything about getting involved? I'd settle for a few hours of pretty awesome sex."

"Same, dude," Lennox moaned. "Same."

Carter stood up, tipping his head toward Lennox as he headed for the door. "I'm down a server tonight, so I gotta get back out there. Chill for as long as you want."

"Thanks, man." Lennox slid down farther on the couch and sighed. "When you get a chance, could you send a beer back here?"

Carter nodded as he stepped out of the office and Lennox was left to enjoy the silence. Campaign season was all about movement and noise. And if he were honest, that was the part he hated most about running for office.

Nothing was more fulfilling than working hard for

the people in his district. But now that he was trying to do that on a larger scale by running for mayor, it meant so much of his focus had to be about how well he performed the campaign song and dance.

"Don't complain," he mumbled. "No one's forcing you to do this."

No one except the trifling son of a bitch who currently sat in the mayor's office. His opponent had done nothing for the five boroughs during his term. Especially certain neighborhoods in Brooklyn that were being gentrified at far too great a rate for the original inhabitants to remain unaffected.

The first twinges of a tension headache prickled at the back of his neck. He closed his eyes and took a few cleansing breaths to bring things back into focus. "Today is a no-work day. Just chill."

Between now, the primary and then Election Day, he wouldn't have too many more of these moments where he could just be and do nothing. So, he'd better take advantage of it while he still could.

The image of the woman with the light brown skin sitting at the bar slid across his mind. She was gorgeous. Even from the bar stool he'd been able to see large, rounded hips and thick thighs. The flex of her calf in those impossibly high black patent leather heels didn't hurt the sexy picture she'd made, either. But when she turned to him with fire smoldering in her eyes, that was when he knew he had to speak to her.

There was an intelligence, a keen awareness there that he couldn't resist. And as gorgeous as the rest of her looked, it was that special something written across her face that read "try Jesus, not me," letting you know she wasn't to be messed with, that made him want to know everything about her.

But now wasn't the time. Not just because she didn't appear to be in the best mood, but because his life was about to turn into chaos. He'd be under the microscope for the next few months. What was it his campaign manager, John, said?

*Don't do anything stupid, keep your dick in your pants, and you might just win this thing.*

A light tap on the door intruded on his thoughts. His friend always had the best timing. A cold beer was just what he needed to get his mind right.

He got to his feet and in two long strides was at the door, swinging it open. "Thanks, man. I was just about—"

His mouth stopped working momentarily when he saw the beautiful woman he'd been obsessing about standing before him, leaning into the doorframe.

"You were just about to what?"

He let his gaze openly slide down her full-figured form and didn't bother to try to hide his appreciation. "I think I should be asking you that. What are you doing back here? Are you lost?"

She shook her head, never once dropping her gaze as she continued to flash her slightly sinful grin.

"Nope," she replied. "Ian is getting slammed out front, so I offered to bring you the beer you ordered. I didn't know it would be you. But I'm not exactly upset it is."

He tilted his head, taking in the full picture of her and trying hard to remember John's edict about keeping his dick in his pants.

"Speaking of not being upset, when we spoke earlier, you didn't seem to be in the best mood."

"A strange man was kind to me for no other reason than he could be. Who knew that kind of courtesy would improve my mood?" She stood up to her full height. In those sexy stilettos he'd admired earlier, the top of her head came to just beneath his chin.

"Since your mood's better, would you like to come in and keep me company?"

"I don't want to intrude."

"You're not," he answered, then stepped aside, letting her in. When she sat down on the couch, he remained standing at the now-closed door.

*This isn't smart, Lennox. You don't know this woman from Adam.*

He didn't. But that didn't seem to stop him from sitting down next to her on the couch.

She handed him an unopened longneck before speaking again. "I told Ian to leave it closed so you could be certain it wasn't tampered with."

Courteous and aware that accepting open drinks from strangers could be hazardous. He was liking her even more.

He didn't respond. He simply took the offered bottle and stack of napkins, twisting the metal cap off and taking a long drink. Was he thirsty? Yeah, but by the way she smiled at him while leaning back and crossing one thick leg over the other, he could see they both knew this was more about distraction than needing a drink.

Lennox put the beer down on a nearby end table and stared at the woman sitting next to him. Trying hard to remember John's warning, he fought with himself about what he should say next. Lennox was in no way afraid to talk to a woman as fine as this. But when you were trying to become the mayor of New York City, you had to think twice about what you said as well as did.

He extended his hand to her, "Thank you, Ms...."

She tilted her head, her sultry gaze sliding down the seated length of him, leaving a fiery burn in its wake. But instead of making him back away like the cautious, levelheaded professional he was supposed to be, it made him lean in closer.

She took his offered hand in a firm grip and smiled. "Angel," she said. "My name's Angel."

"Angel is a lovely name. It's my pleasure to make your acquaintance."

She continued to smile at him, holding his hand and letting her thumb pass over his knuckle. It wasn't necessarily an overt gesture of attraction. But coupled with the flash of fire he saw in her eyes, he was pretty sure they were vibing on the same wavelength.

"Well," she said, breaking the silence. "I don't want to interrupt you any further. I suppose if you're back here and not at the bar, you probably weren't looking for company."

She stood up, and he followed suit, stepping closer to her than he probably should have considering he didn't know anything about her beyond her name.

"I did come back here to get away from the crowd. But that's not the reason you should leave."

She folded her arms, pushing her full, round breasts up, and he couldn't find enough decency anywhere in him to look away.

"I'm not sure I get your meaning," she responded. "What's the reason I should leave?"

He hesitated for a moment, pulling his lip between his teeth to keep the words on the tip of his tongue from spilling out of his mouth.

"Aww, don't get shy now, Len. Speak your peace."

He nodded, loving the fierceness she wore like a second skin.

"You should leave because I'm tempted to find out if this thing that makes me want to bend you over that desk is mutual. Because if it is, I don't think I have enough give-a-damn to ignore it."

There, he'd given her the truth. And if she was smart, she'd take her leave, and this would never become more than a little flirting in the back of a bar.

But when she stepped into his space, so close that all he needed to do was shift slightly and his body would be pressed against hers, he groaned.

"You'd better know what you're doing, Angel."

She narrowed her gaze as her full lips curved into a sultry smile. "Is Len short for Leonard?"

Her question seemed out of place, but instead of using that brief moment as an excuse to step away, he shook his head. "No, it's short for Lennox."

"Good." She moved in closer, wrapping her hand around the base of his neck. "I'd like to make sure I'm calling you by your proper name if this ends up being as good as I hope it will be."

Lennox's entire body tightened. Given her provocative words, coupled with the firm yet tender feel of her hand against his bare flesh, it was a wonder he didn't explode right then and there.

"Make sure you know what you want, Angel." His eyes locked with hers, finding a blaze of fire that rivaled the inferno burning inside him.

"I always know what I'm doing, Lennox. I was just waiting for you to catch up so I could get what I want."

He smoothed strong hands up her sides and placed a firm grip on her waist, pulling her against him. He waited a second to see if there was any resistance, but when she leaned into him, pressing herself against his already twitching cock, all he could do was smile.

"And just what is it that you want from me?"

She tilted her head with her sexy grin still caressing her lips. "A one-time offer for you to—how'd you put it?—find out if this thing that makes me want you to bend me over that desk is mutual."

He groaned as he positioned his lips less than an inch away from hers. All it would take to set this off was the slightest lean and he'd finally know what those plush pillows felt like pressed against his mouth.

"That's all it can be, Angel. I don't have room in my life for more at the moment."

"No worries, Lennox." The way she said his name with such authority made his heart beat harder against his chest. "I've had an unusually difficult day and a little mindless fun with you would certainly help me unwind. But beyond this moment, I don't have the spoons to heap another thing onto my plate right now. So, can you handle a few moments of bliss with me and nothing more?"

He stepped around her slowly, walking to the door and twisting the lock to make certain they weren't interrupted.

He stared at her, looking for any signs of unease or discomfort. When she smiled, lifting a coy brow and leaning back casually against Carter's mostly empty desk.

"You ready to do this, Lennox?"

"Hell, yes."

It was the last coherent thought he had before he stalked toward her and finally allowed his lips to touch hers. Fire shot through him. When she slipped her fingers around the sensitive skin of his neck, cupping it, pulling him closer, making sure he couldn't escape, it was an accelerant that made the hungry flames licking at every inch of his skin burn brighter and faster.

She slipped her hand beneath the lapels of his jacket, pushing it off his shoulders and down his arms. She broke the kiss, staring at him as if she needed to commit every line on his face to memory. He stared back, needing to do the same.

Their movements quickly turned frantic and desperate. While he was pulling up her pencil skirt, hitching it up just enough that he could freely lodge himself between the cradle of her legs, she was unknotting his tie and unbuttoning his shirt. Then they switched, him working his way down her buttoned shirt, splaying the two flaps to take in the perfect vision of her luscious breasts in a breathtakingly sexy black lace demi bra while she unbuckled his belt and pants, slipping her warm hand inside and boldly cupping his sex.

She looked up at him, winking as she gave him a squeeze, and everything in his world narrowed into the feel of her hot palm searing his flesh. The tension of his day bled out of him, replaced by the hungry tension of arousal.

This was exactly what he needed. Fun with a partner who knew what the hell she wanted and wasn't afraid to grab it. Literally.

He moaned as he gave in to the tantalizing slide of her closed palm up his length. He allowed her a few more strokes. Then he pulled her hand away, placing it flat on the desk and leaning in to steal a desperate kiss.

"That feels great. But too much more of that and neither of us will get what we want."

She nodded, tugging her skirt up a little higher, wrapping her legs around him. "Then quit stalling, let's get to it."

Never taking his eyes off her, he slid his hand over her smooth, tanned skin until his thumb rested at the juncture between her thighs. He hesitated for a second, taking her chin between the fingers of his free hand.

"Are you sure this is still what you want?"

She took the hand he had latched on her thigh, moving it over her mound and pressing against it until he was cupping her sex with his whole hand.

"I'm sure."

He let out the breath he was holding. He pushed aside the black patch of lace covering her, finding slick heat beneath it. The moment his fingers made contact with her flesh, they both gave into a deep and satisfying moan, its vibrations shaking through his entire being.

He latched his mouth on to hers as his fingers continued their exploration, parting her flesh and slipping one, then two fingers inside of her. She rewarded him with a slow swivel of her hips and wrapped her arms around his neck, using him as her anchor as she rode his fingers, hanging on to the very edge of what he hoped would be a memorable orgasm with the greatest show of resolve he'd ever witnessed.

Determined to break her, he swiped his thumb over her clit with his fingers still buried inside of her and it was the final chink in her armor. Every place where their bodies touched, she wrapped herself around him, squeezing him in what had to be the most sensual embrace he'd ever experienced.

Watching her come heightened his arousal, his length hard and insistent against his abdomen, aching for the same chance at release he'd just given her.

When she finally came down from her climax, he untangled himself from her long enough to find the condom he always kept in his wallet. He wasted no time pushing his clothes down just enough and slid the condom on as quickly as he could.

Sheathed, he placed himself at her opening, wrapping his arm around her waist while his opposite hand traveled up to her breasts, tweaking one pebbled nipple between his fingers as he slid slowly home.

And that's exactly what bottoming out into the depths of her body felt like.

They fit better than lock and key. No awkward groping, no off-beat rhythm. From the moment his flesh touched hers they were in sync with each other's movements.

It didn't matter how fast and hard he thrust, creating the beautiful slapping sound of slick flesh against flesh. It didn't matter how slowly he slid in and out, taking the time to savor her kisses, worshipping her mouth as well as her body. Whatever their tempo, she was right there with him, providing the answer to every movement he initiated.

And when she clenched around him, drawing out his orgasm as she succumbed to a second climax of her own, their mutual release was the perfect end to the moment they'd shared. The moment that couldn't be repeated.

Spent, trying to regain enough energy to pull his body away from hers and the dexterity he needed to right his clothing, he thanked all the stars in the sky that this would never happen again. Because if it was that good when they were perfect strangers, it frightened him how good it would really be if they knew more than each other's first names. Her sex could be addictive. And right now, he didn't have the luxury of being strung out on anyone. Not if he wanted to win.

When he was finally able to slow his labored breathing, he pulled out, looking down to remove the condom when shock mixed with equal parts fear spilled down his spine.

"What's wrong?"

When he looked up at her, he could see his panic reflected in her deep brown eyes. He swallowed, finally finding the courage to speak three chilling words.

"The condom broke."

# Three

"Lennox, did you hear me?"

The sound of his campaign manager's voice snatched him from his thoughts.

"Len?" John Christos, a tall, lean man of Greek decent with almost black hair and blue eyes, stared at him, waiting for an answer.

"I'm sorry, John. I'm just preoccupied."

"With what?"

*Oh, nothing. Just sitting here wondering whether I impregnated a stranger four weeks ago.*

Lennox closed his eyes as the thought dragged across his mind. When he met John's assessing gaze, he turned in his chair to face the window.

"Nothing I care to share at the moment. Let's get back to work."

When he swiveled back to John, he saw a strange mix of pity and compassion painted across the man's face.

"Lennox, I know these last four weeks have been brutal. The nonstop rallies, the appearances, the debates, all while still handling your duties as city councilman. It's a lot. But all the work you've put in has led to a twelve-point lead in the polls. The primary is yours if you can just hold out for a little longer."

He dragged a deep breath in through his nose, trying to quell all the alarm bells ringing in the back of his head. Everything John stated was fact. If his campaign kept up its current momentum, he would be the next mayor of New York City. Which was why he was so pissed that he'd let a moment of weakness possibly derail that.

"You can do this, man," John continued. "I don't back lost causes. If I agreed to run your campaign, you know it's because I believe you'd win."

Lennox met John's gaze with a smile. The man was known as the best in the business for that very reason. Lennox was lucky to have him running the show. Which was why he knew he also needed to come clean. If this shit blew up in his face, blindsiding John wouldn't help Lennox or his campaign.

"I know I can do this," he whispered. "But I don't know if I'll get the chance."

John's brow furrowed as he straightened in his seat. "What happened?"

"About a month ago, I met a woman at Carter's place."

John took a sharp breath. "Why do I already know I'm not going to like how this story ends?"

"Because you're smart," Lennox answered. "Smarter than I was."

"Please tell me it was consensual, and she wasn't an employee, or in any way directly connected to your campaign."

Lennox's body tensed as he glared at John.

"What?" He spat the words through clenched teeth. "You really think so little of me?"

"It's not about what I think. It's about how she felt and whether or not she believes you violated her boundaries. So, I'll ask you again. Was the sex consensual?"

As offended as Lennox was, he realized John was right. It wasn't about him. It was about whether his partner felt safe in that moment.

"It was. We both verbally agreed to the sex before, during and after the act."

"But?"

"The condom broke."

John's stiff posture relaxed a little, and his stern expression was softened by compassion.

"So, you're worried about a health scare and unwanted pregnancy?"

Lennox rubbed at the dull throb starting to thump at his temples.

"I had blood work done a couple of days ago. My doc says everything came back negative but wants me to be tested at the three and sixth-month markers to be certain."

"And the pregnancy?"

"This woman was a perfect stranger, John. Other than her first name, I have no idea who she is. I gave her all of my contact information. I told her to call me if our time together resulted in pregnancy."

"Has she?"

Lennox shook his head slowly, wishing the lack of contact from his mystery Angel eased his mind as much as it should.

"Have you called her?"

"She wouldn't give me her info."

John stood, running his hand through his short dark waves before he started pacing. This was classic problem-solver John. He thought better when he was moving, and with all Lennox had just dropped in his lap, the man probably needed to run a couple of laps to figure out how to fix this situation Lennox found himself in.

"Doesn't Carter's lounge require membership? Even if you're a guest of a guest, they have to submit ID, right?"

Lennox nodded. "True, but I'm trying hard not to ask my friend to violate the privacy of one of his members for my personal issues."

"So, unless this stranger tells you she's carrying your baby…"

"I'll never know."

John stared back at him, his face relaying the words the man had yet to speak.

*You are so screwed.*

"Cousin?"

Amara had just parked in front of Devereaux Manor when her phone rang. Turning the ignition off, she settled back into her seat before responding to her beloved cousin Stephan. These weekly phone calls had become their new tradition since Ace was rushed to the hospital last month.

"He's still with us, Stephan."

There was an audible sigh of relief on the other end of the line.

"I speak to Uncle Ace on our weekly Zoom calls. He never lets on to how he's really doing." Stephan's voice was barely a whisper but the worry in this tone came through loud and clear. "I promised him I'd be home in time for Trey and Jeremiah's wedding next week. Do you think I should get home sooner?"

"Steph, if you can get away, I'd tell you to get home now. That old man is a fighter, but I don't know how much longer he can keep this up."

The line went quiet for so long, she looked at her screen to make sure they hadn't been disconnected.

"Steph, you still there?"

"Yeah," he answered, sounding slightly distracted. "I'm just making some arrangements."

"Want me to send the family jet for you?"

She heard keys tapping on his end, followed by what sounded like shuffling papers.

"No," he answered quickly. "The jet is in New York. It'll take seven hours to get here and another seven to get me back home. There's a commercial flight leaving in two hours. I'll be in New York by eleven tonight your time."

She couldn't help but smile. Out of all of her cousins, Stephan was the most like Ace. Strong, decisive and able to make an effective plan even in the face of crisis. If her cousin had wanted it, she was certain Ace would've chosen him as his second-in-command. Not that Jeremiah and Trey weren't equally qualified. But the way Stephan always figured out what the best path was in an instant, that was something he inherited from their uncle.

"I'm glad you're coming back, Steph. There's a lot of upheaval going on and your calming presence will definitely help."

Truer words had never been spoken. Amara had made a huge mess of things. Sleeping with Lennox Carlisle was a huge mistake.

*You knew that when you entered that office at The Vault. Why would you do this in the first place?*

Hurt.

That was the simple answer. Her grandfather's lack of faith in her leadership skills found the wound she'd secretly hidden all these years. As much as her grandfather didn't believe she measured up to her mother as a lawyer, deep down, Amara had always feared it was true. And having her grandfather snatch the one thing that would've proven she'd surpassed her mother's successes made her ache for comfort in the worst way.

She'd thought the drink, the pretzels, and the hot wings would be enough to make her feel better. But when Lennox offered her kindness and unquestioning support, she'd forgotten all the reasons she should stay away from the man and given into her need to just feel good for once in that moment.

Fortunately, she never had to see Lennox again since she'd been taken off the deal. Otherwise, this bad situation she'd created for herself would be a whole lot worse.

"You mean with our long-lost cousin and new CEO?

Is Trey a problem? 'Cause you know I don't have an issue coming in and wrecking shop."

A hardy, deep laugh slipped through her lips. Considering all the stress the family had been under recently, it felt good to let go for a brief moment and enjoy Stephan's sense of humor.

"Trey is actually kinda badass. I like her a lot. I think you will, too. But just so you know, you might wanna watch how you talk about her. Jeremiah is pretty much sprung. He might not take too lightly to you coming after his woman."

Stephan chuckled, and Amara felt her smile widen. "Listen, Jeremiah knows the most important trait of surviving in the Devereaux clan is having a thick skin. If Trey hasn't already learned that lesson, she's about to get schooled."

"She's good people, Steph. She's also really good for the company and Ace."

"Unlike my mama, you mean?"

That was an understatement. Martha had attempted to steal Devereaux Inc. from Ace. And as angry as she was about losing to Trey and Jeremiah, Amara had a bad feeling the woman wasn't done waging war on the rest of the family yet.

"She blames Ace for a lot of her pain, Stephan. You know that. If you're coming home, maybe stop in and talk to her. Tell her Randall's death and your leaving wasn't his fault. Try to get her to see Ace and settle this nonsense before it's too late."

Losing Stephan's older brother had been a blow to the entire family. But to their mother, Martha, it had decimated her life.

"I'm coming to New York to see my uncle and attend my cousins' wedding. My mother's nonsense will have to wait until another day," he said in a clipped tone. "I'll hit you up when I land, Cousin. Tell that old man I'm on my way."

"I will, Cousin. See you soon."

She dropped her phone into her purse and stepped out of her car. As she looked up at the grand white pillars at the front entrance of the mansion, a familiar ease spread through her. Although she and her parents hadn't lived at Devereaux Manor, she'd spent so much time there growing up, learning from her grandfather and Ace as they built Devereaux Inc. into an unstoppable force that would last for generations.

She'd never been happier than the times she'd sat at those two wise men's feet, soaking up all they had to teach a young, impressionable girl about dominating the business world.

But today, her shoulders were heavy with worry as she considered that the dynamic of her family could quite possibly change forever, and she was powerless to stop it.

*Get yourself together. You've got to be strong for him.*

After taking another moment to compose herself and still the tremors that threatened to reveal just how afraid she was, she rang the bell.

A few seconds later, Ace's home health aide Ms. Alicia's bright smile greeted her as she ushered Amara inside.

"Ms. Amara," she beamed. "Your uncle was just asking about you a little while ago."

"I guess that's why my ears were burning." Amara smiled and gave the woman and tight hug. Alicia had been with Ace only a couple months but she was already an irreplaceable fixture in the family. "Is Uncle Ace up for visitors?"

Alicia shook her head. "Visitors? No. Family? Always. You can go right on upstairs to his bedroom. He sent the rest of the family out to get some rest. You'll have him all to yourself until the others start trickling back in."

Amara gave Alicia another hug and walked upstairs, tapping on the heavy wood door before she slowly slid it open.

There, in the middle of the room, Ace sat up in the king-size four-poster bed that seemed way too large for his frail form. He looked so much smaller, so delicate. It was heartbreaking. She was about ready to collapse into a puddle of tears until she saw the bright sparkle of joy and mischief in the older man's eyes and suddenly, she forgot about his infirmity. In those eyes, she saw the strength and love that had carried her throughout her life, and somehow that was enough to help her hold on to her composure.

*"Tío,"* she half sang as she walked toward him with her arms stretched wide, *"te extrañé."*

To make sure that she was fluent in Spanish, her Afro-Cuban father had spoken exclusively to her in his native language when she was a child. To support that decision, Ace learned to speak conversational Spanish so he could converse with his only grandniece.

"You just saw me yesterday." He waved a dismissive hand in the air. "How can you miss me already?"

She sat down on the edge of his bed and he gathered her into his arms. She could feel his bones as he hugged her, which saddened her more than she could say. But the blessing of still being able to be held and loved by this man kept the shadows of grief away.

"You are my favorite uncle," she beamed. "I miss you every moment we're apart."

He pulled away from her, placing his long hands on her cheeks and caressing the skin there with his withered thumbs.

"And that is exactly why you will always be my favorite grandniece."

She lifted her eyebrow, knowing full well he told every single family member they were his favorite, but still loving the special feeling it gave her every time she heard him say it.

"You'd better not let Lyric hear you say that. You know she thinks she's your favorite."

He placed a gentle kiss on her forehead and leaned back against the headboard of his bed.

"She's my favorite niece. You're my favorite grandniece. There's no comparison."

"You're very lucky I'm you're only grandniece." She wagged a finger at him. "Otherwise, I might be offended."

He chuckled softly, patting her hand as he stared into her eyes. "I love all my babies. Nothing makes me happier than all of you being around. Having four of you here has done my heart glad."

She could see the slight bit of sadness twinkling in his muted brown gaze.

"He's coming home, Uncle."

She didn't have to say who *he* was. The spark of acknowledgment in Ace's eyes and the resulting expectant smile said he knew exactly who she was talking about.

"Is he?"

She nodded. "Yes, Stephan will be on a plane in two hours. He should probably get to Brooklyn sometime around midnight." She lifted her brow as she tilted her head. "He would've been here earlier if you hadn't told him to stay in Paris."

Ace squeezed her hand and gave her a timid smile filled with remorse. "I knew if I asked, he'd come. There's so much pain for him here. I didn't want my boy to suffer just so I could have the pleasure of holding him in my arms one last time."

His words chipped away at her resolve, and she couldn't hold back the hot tears that spilled onto her cheek and slid down her face. With trembling hands, she held his face and made sure his gaze locked with hers.

"Here me now, Jordan Dylan Devereaux. You're worthy of any sacrifice we have to make to keep you happy and proud. You've been the bedrock of this family and championed for each one of us. There isn't anything you could ask of us that we wouldn't give you. You're that important. *Lo entiendes?*"

He tugged her into his embrace, stroking her hair as he had when she was a child in need of comfort. *"Sí sobrina,"* he whispered softly in her ear. "I am such a lucky man to have the five of you in my life. When each of you were given to me, I promised Alva I'd do everything in my power to protect you, love you and support you in any way you needed me to, all in exchange for your happiness. Trey and Jeremiah are taken care of. After speaking to Lyric, I think she might be halfway there herself with that producer friend of hers, Josiah. I'm especially happy about that because she was widowed so young when Randall died, too young to be alone for the rest of her life. Now it's just you and Stephan."

She sat up, gently pulling out of his embrace and looking at him with playful suspicion. "Uncle Ace…"

He shook his head. "I know you don't need a man to complete you. You are fierce, powerful and one of the most beautiful creatures to ever walk on this earth."

Amara couldn't help smiling. Even frail and sick, the old man was a slick flatterer.

"I don't want you to have someone because I think you're incomplete," he continued. "I want you to have someone who will do for you what I have always done— love you, support you, protect you."

He rubbed her hand and smiled back at her. "So, niece, if you want me to remember how much I'm loved, you have to do me this one favor. Remember the love I've had for you your whole life, and when it comes again in a new form, recognize it and let it in."

Every part of the independent woman in her wanted to rebuff his words. But somehow, coming from him, coming from the depths of the love he'd always shown her, she couldn't deny how tempting Ace made love sound.

She took a breath and closed her eyes to gather her strength before continuing. "Don't worry about me, Uncle Ace. I'll be just fine. Besides, my work for Devereaux Inc. keeps me so busy, there's very little chance of me finding the kind of love you want for me."

He readjusted the pillows behind his back before responding. "Speaking of work, I talked to David."

Amara shook her head. "Uncle Ace..."

"Let me finish, chile. David was wrong and I told him so. There's no one who's worked harder than you have. You deserve to be his successor."

She huffed, trying her best not to take her frustration out on her beloved uncle. "My grandfather has made his decision, and he obviously doesn't have faith in me. There's no use arguing about it."

"Don't be so sure. As much as your grandfather accuses you of being unable to see the big picture, I reminded him of a few times throughout his career when he acted much in the same way. Give him some time, niece. He's a little slow on the uptake sometimes, but he eventually gets there."

She shook her head and gave him a soft smile. "I came here to check on you and give you comfort, and here you are making me feel better. How does that work?"

He chuckled and patted her hand. "It doesn't matter if I'm sick. It's still my job to take care of my babies. It's a responsibility I will always fulfill."

She picked up his withered yet remarkably strong hand and kissed it. "I love you, Uncle."

"Not more than I love you, baby."

# Four

"Amara?"

At the sound of her grandfather's voice, she lifted her gaze to find him standing in her office doorway.

"Do you have a few minutes to talk?"

There was something about the almost solemn quality to his voice that made fear wrap around her spine, pulling her straight up out of her chair.

"Is everything all right? Is it Uncle Ace?"

The tight lines of her grandfather's face relaxed and he rushed into the room, standing next to her and pulling her into his arms.

"No, baby. Ace is still with us. I'm sorry if I worried you."

Relief bled through her. Knowing you were losing someone in no way meant you were prepared for their eventual departure. And this moment proved to her she would probably never be ready to get that terrible news.

He released her and gave her a wry smile as she nodded and returned to her seat, gesturing for him to take the chair on the other side of her desk.

"What's going on, Granddaddy?"

"Your uncle ending up in the hospital was a reality check for me. I don't have a lot of time left with my brother, and I want to spend whatever remainder I have at his side. I know I accused you of being too impetuous to be my successor."

"Has your opinion of me changed?"

He chuckled and shook his head. "No. You are impetuous. But you're also one hell of a lawyer and you know Devereaux Inc. like the back of your hand. I would like to see you temper your approaches a little. However, that shouldn't be a reason to keep you from the position you've clearly earned. We have a solid team, and you're smart enough to listen to them to figure out when caution is needed."

She felt a glimmer of hope. Too afraid to let it grow for fear of disappointment, she sat up straighter in her chair and braced herself for his next words.

"What are you saying, Granddaddy?"

He took a breath and stood, extending his hand for her to shake. "I'm saying, I'm taking a leave of absence to spend time with my brother and making you acting lead counsel of Devereaux Inc."

Amara tugged her lip between her teeth, fighting desperately to restrain her show of excitement so she didn't end up jumping up and down and clapping like a seal.

"I promise to make you proud, Granddaddy. You won't regret this."

"I know you will. Consider this your audition for the job. It's your chance to show me you're the best choice for the position. Don't blow it, Amara."

"I won't."

He smiled at her, but she could still see the wariness in his eyes. He didn't have to worry she wouldn't mess this up.

"Good. Now, cut out some time in your schedule to come have a cup coffee with me so I can get you caught up on this Falcon deal. You're set to meet with Councilman Lennox Carlisle tomorrow morning."

Amara's body tightened and the bottom of her stomach felt like it dropped a few stories. Instantly images of her and Lennox locked in a quick and dirty embrace flashed across her mind.

"Are you all right?" Her grandfather's concern dropped the curtain on her memories. Her hotheadedness had made her indulge in petty and self-indulgent revenge that was now coming back to bite her on the ass.

The responsible thing to do would've been to come clean. She knew this. But when she looked into her grandfather's face, she couldn't reveal the truth. She'd worked so hard to get what she wanted, to prove her worth. No way was she allowing a momentary lapse in judgment destroy all her dreams and hard work.

She'd spent four weeks worried that she might be pregnant. Her period arriving—albeit lighter, earlier and shorter than usual, a fact she attributed to her stressing out over the situation—should've been her opportunity to let this go. But now, the universe was serving her just desserts, making her face the mess she'd made.

"Nothing's wrong. I'll have my assistant check my calendar and we'll set a time." She looked up at him with a grateful smile on her lips. "Thank you, Granddaddy."

He leaned down and pressed a gentle kiss on her cheek before leaving the room. She stood in the middle of her office thinking back to her time with Lennox, pushing back the fear she could feel rising from the pit of her stomach. She couldn't let it overwhelm her. Not now.

She put her head down on her desk and closed her eyes as she tried to get a hold of herself. With nothing but work to connect them now, she had to focus on the job at hand. Because no one, not even the sexy man who'd brought her to earth-shattering climaxes in a short amount of time, would keep her from doing what she did best: protecting Devereaux Inc.'s interests.

A loud knock made Amara jump in her chair. She blinked a few times until she realized she was still in her office, sitting at her desk.

"So, you get the big promotion you've been working your butt off for and you celebrate by falling asleep at your desk, Cousin?"

Amara followed the familiar voice until she found Stephan seated on the edge of her desk.

"Technically, I'm just the stand-in while Granddaddy is on leave. Besides, there's no time for celebration when you've got as much work on your desk as I do." She stood up and stretched, then grabbed two armfuls of the man sitting on her desk.

"Cousin," she crooned. "I missed you. I wish you were here under better circumstances."

They hugged tightly, hanging on as if they were much-needed lifelines for each other. "Have you seen Uncle Ace since you got in last night or did you go straight to your place?"

"I stayed at Devereaux Manor last night. I plan to stay there for the duration of my trip. I've missed two years' worth of moments with Uncle Ace because of bullshit. I'm not going to miss any more of the time he has left."

Amara pulled back to look into Stephan's dark eyes and ached at the sadness she saw there. He'd lost his only brother, Randall, two years ago, and now he was poised to lose another loved one so soon after.

"I can only imagine Uncle Ace was thrilled when he saw you."

"Uncle David and Ace were asleep when I let myself in. I grabbed a quick bite from the kitchen and spent the night curled up in the chair at Ace's bedside. It wasn't the greatest thing for my back after a transatlantic flight. But getting to see the big grin on Uncle Ace's face when he saw me, that was worth every ache I have."

She laid a hand over his and smiled. "You're such a good man, Stephan."

He just nodded, silently looking her up and down.

"I thought I'd see if you wanted to have dinner with me, but all you seem ready for is an evening nap. Everything okay? You not getting enough rest at home?"

She went to speak but found herself fighting off a

big yawn. "I sleep fine. I don't know why I'm so tired all of a sudden."

She'd never been one to take naps. But she yearned for at least twenty minutes more of the impromptu catnap Stephan had interrupted.

"I guess it's the stress of prepping for this Falcon deal. I closed my eyes for a minute, and I wake up to you giving me a hard time."

He waved a dismissive hand at her. "Girl please, since when are you stressed about doing deals? You've been beating folks outta their coins since we were in diapers. Remember when you convinced Ace that taking us to the new ice cream shop downtown was an educational outing because we'd get to explore your scientific hypothesis that black cherry was indeed tastier than strawberry?"

She looked up at him, basking in the glow of his warm smile. "A theory I still stand by, thank you very much."

"My point is—" he poked his finger against her shoulder as he laughed "—if you can do that, this Falcon deal should be a breeze. Stop stressing and come treat your handsome cousin to dinner like he does for you when you visit him in Paris."

"I guess I can feed you."

He jutted his jaw in her direction. "You'd better. Usually, Jeremiah or Ace would have a full spread waiting for me the moment I entered Devereaux Manor. Last night, I had a ham sandwich. And it wasn't even hand-carved ham. I'm talking your run-of-the-mill deli slices. You know I'm too boujee for all that. You need to take pity on me."

"Poor baby," she cooed. "Let's go get you something suitable to eat while I give you all the family updates and you tell me about all the fine men in Paris that are begging for the slightest bit of your attention. I need to live vicariously through you."

After nearly blowing her life to shreds by sleeping with Lennox, that was the only kind of action Amara was interested in. Stephan had always been able to make her laugh and keep her mind off her problems. More than ever, she needed him to use his superpower tonight.

Because tomorrow would come all too quickly, and she'd finally have to deal with this very messy situation she'd created. Resigned to her plan to distract herself, she stood, grabbing her Louis Vuitton OnTheGo MM tote before looping her arm through Stephan's and giving him a wide grin. "It really is good to have you home, Cousin."

# Five

Amara sat in the back seat of the platinum Mercedes-Maybach tapping her fingers against the armrest as her driver took them over the Brooklyn Bridge. A few minutes later, they were weaving through Manhattan traffic, past City Hall, until he pulled up to the curb in front of 250 Broadway.

She grabbed her briefcase and gave the chauffer's shoulder a squeeze. "It's a bus stop. No need to get out, Mr. Parker. I don't want you getting a ticket."

She watched the momentary flash of resistance in his eye. He'd worked for Devereaux Inc. probably since before she was born, and he absolutely hated it whenever she opened the door for herself and hopped out.

Today, however, she had too much restless energy and she needed to work it out of her system. She'd use the few extra seconds alone to collect herself before she faced off with Lennox Carlisle.

As she approached the entrance to the office building, she took a breath, smoothing her hand over any imaginary wrinkles in her black strapless jumpsuit. She'd paired it with a white, wide-collared blazer, and black-and-white color block heels, presenting the perfect picture of a business executive with just enough flair to be noticed and not ridiculed.

Her clothes were her armor. The first thing people saw that showed them exactly who they were dealing with: a boss who had the power of Devereaux Inc. behind her.

A quick glance at her reflection in the glass doors and she knew she looked like a force to be reckoned with. But inside, she felt like a fidgety intern nervous about her first round of negotiations. That wouldn't do. Especially not in front of a man who knew what she looked like naked.

Well, partially naked, if she remembered correctly. And she definitely remembered that night correctly.

Those few minutes in that secluded office at The Vault had been the best sex of her life. Hot, uninhibited and so damn good she could still feel his scorching touch.

She shook her head, forcing the fluttering nerves in her stomach to subside as she squared her shoulders and made her way inside. A short time later, she was opening the door into the reception area of his office where she was greeted by an Asian man in his mid to late twenties with a welcoming smile.

"Hello, I'm Thomas, welcome to Councilman Carlisle's office. How may I help you?"

"Good afternoon," she said, offering a pleasant smile. "Amara Devereaux-Rodriguez on behalf of Devereaux Incorporated. I'm here to see the councilman."

Thomas nodded and stood, directing her to a small waiting area. "Please have a seat, Ms. Devereaux-Rodriguez. I'll let the councilman know you're here."

She sat down and placed her briefcase on the floor next to her, then crossed her legs to get comfortable. She took in the room. It looked like any other municipal office in the city, with its assembly-line art covering the white walls and gray metal desks and filing cabinets.

"Ms. Devereaux-Rodriguez." Thomas's voice pulled her attention away from her thoughts. "I'm afraid the councilman is in the middle of urgent business. He says he's not certain when he'll be able to receive you. Perhaps we should reschedule for a later date."

She tilted her head to the side and watched Thomas. His face was relaxed, with just enough faux concern that he appeared remorseful for the message he was delivering. But he didn't know who he was up against.

"Oh, I'm fine with waiting. I've cleared my entire calendar this afternoon just to talk to the councilman. Please tell him I'll be here whenever he's free to see me." She leaned down to pull her iPad mini out of her briefcase. She opened the keyboard folio case and positioned the device on top of her thighs, preparing to tap at the tiny keys.

When she looked up again, she watched Thomas nervously swallow. She gave him a knowing wink before returning her attention to her tablet.

*Sucks to be you, Thomas. Go tell your boss I called his bluff.*

* * *

"Sir, I don't think the Devereaux Inc. rep is gonna fall for your usual diversion tactics. She's basically set up shop in the waiting area as if she plans to be here all day."

Lennox groaned as he leaned back in his chair. He didn't have time for this. He was knee-deep in campaign work, which wasn't going well because he was too distracted thinking about Angel. Would he ever see her again? Would she be willing to see him again? And the most distracting thought of all, did they conceive a child together four weeks ago?

His mood taking a decided plunge, he glared at Thomas. "I don't care if she sets up shop or not. Let her. I'll wait her out. Eventually she'll get annoyed enough, or hungry enough to leave."

He returned his attention to his computer screen, silently dismissing Thomas. He knew what this rep wanted, and there was no way in hell she was getting it. Devereaux Inc. was in league with Falcon Development, and he wouldn't let them push another resident out of Brooklyn to gentrify it. Nope, not today, not ever.

New fire sparked in his chest, and he was able to clear his mind of all distraction. He set about handling the people's business, checking one thing at a time off his to-do list.

By the time his stomach reminded him that he'd skipped lunch, he looked out his window to find dusk settling over the city. A quick look at his watch and he realized he'd been working three hours straight.

Lennox buzzed for Thomas to come to his office.

When he did, he was carrying a large pizza box with a couple of paper bags on top.

"Is that from Artichoke Pizza?" His stomach growled at the thought of his favorite pizza place. When Thomas confirmed with a grin and a nod, Lennox moaned in anticipation. "This is why I will never fire you. You always anticipate what I need before I can even ask for it. Thanks, Thomas."

There was a mischievous grin on Thomas's face that made Lennox suddenly aware he was in trouble.

"Don't thank me," Thomas replied. "Thank the rep from Devereaux Inc. When she saw we were all working late, she placed an order for the entire office."

Lennox took the pizza box, too hungry to care who'd ordered it. He opened the box, seeing the darkened brown crust of a well-done artichoke and extra-cheese pie.

"At least you told her what to order."

Thomas shook his head. "No, she didn't ask me what to order. Apparently, she's done some research on you." He pointed to the two bags Lennox had pulled off the top of the box.

Lennox opened one of the bags to see two cans of Dr. Pepper in one, and a bag of buttery garlic knots in the other.

He narrowed his gaze as he looked up at Thomas. He was intrigued now, which was exactly what he'd bet the Devereaux rep wanted. He chuckled to himself, amused by the lengths to which this person would go for an audience with him.

"Tell her she's got until I finish my last can of Dr. Pepper to speak her piece."

If the grin on Thomas's face was any indication, he was certainly enjoying this game of chess between Lennox and the Devereaux rep. He nodded and headed for the door.

Without preamble, Lennox tore into a slice, folding the triangle in half like any proper New Yorker would. That first bite was heaven, and he didn't censor the almost obscene moan of sheer gratification that slipped from his lips.

"I hope you saved a slice for me?"

He looked up and choked. Once his coughing fit stopped, he swallowed the food in his mouth and grimaced as it hit his stomach like concrete cinderblocks.

"Angel?"

She smiled, stepping closer to him and extending a hand. "Amara Angel Devereaux-Rodriguez, lead counsel and negotiator for Devereaux Incorporated. Good to see you again, Lennox."

# Six

Amara steeled herself against Lennox's cold glare. She hadn't exactly expected him to welcome her into his office with open arms once he saw who she was. But the hard anger she saw creeping into his eyes surprised her.

"You?"

*And here we go.*

"I prefer Amara. But yes, it's me. If we're done with the reintroduction, perhaps we can focus on business."

He stood, splaying his fingers on the long conference table in the middle of the room. The angles in his face were sharp, and she was sure she'd cut herself on them if she were foolish enough to try to touch him.

"Business? You have the audacity to saunter into my office to talk business on a major deal after screwing me senseless under an assumed name?"

"Lennox," she said firmly, trying to get a handle on the situation. "If you would just calm down—"

"Calm down?" He spat out the words as he stood to his full height and closed the distance between the two of them. "Unless you're going to tell me you didn't know who I was when you let me bend you over Carter's desk, I don't think there's a chance of me calming down. So, *Amara*, is that the case, or is it safe for me to assume I was set up?"

He watched her for the slightest inkling of guilt or remorse. But what he found in the depths of her dark brown eyes was fire and strength. It was the same power he'd witnessed the one and only time they'd previously met. Its lure had seeped into his blood and made him do something incredibly stupid that could cost him everything. And even now, when he was pissed off beyond all recognition, he could still feel the thrum of arousal coursing through his body as she stood before him, calm and unbothered by his ire.

"Well, are you going to answer me? Or should I take your silence as your official response?"

"The answer is yes and no."

A derisive chuckle escaped his throat as he crossed his arms. "Well, I can't wait to hear this story. It's gotta be a good one if you think you're going to justify your actions."

She lifted a questioning brow as she tilted her head. "My actions? As I remember it, I didn't take anything that wasn't freely given. I was sitting at the bar, and you approached me."

He slowly shook his head from side to side while

keeping his eyes locked on hers. "That is a weak-ass argument, and you know it. It doesn't matter who approached whom first. What does matter is you knew who I was, and you let me sex you anyway."

He saw a slight chip in her composed facade and, for just a second, he wanted to take back his harsh words and comfort her. But then he reminded himself that he was the victim in this situation, and he had a right to be mad as hell.

"I want to know why? Were you trying to set me up for some sort of extortion scheme?"

She took a deep breath, smoothing her hand against her curls that were pulled into a severe bun. After knowing what those curls looked like wild and free, what they felt like against his skin and between his fingers, it offended him to see them locked away under the guise of professionalism.

"I knew who you were." Her statement had a matter-of-fact quality to it that both soothed him and pissed him off. It calmed him because the lawyer in him liked facts. They were easier and less messy to deal with. But the human part of him, the man who'd had the pleasure of knowing what sliding inside of her body felt like, raged at the fact she could speak about their encounter with so little emotion.

"I'd had a really rough day at work. My boss denied me a promotion and basically affirmed what I've always known to be true—he didn't think I was good enough to do the job. That's especially hard to swallow when your boss is your grandfather, and the only person he thinks is worthy is the same person he's always compared you to, your mother.

"I was feeling raw and angry and then you walked in and you were kind to me and you agreed with my perspective without knowing any of the details. After a blow like the one I'd suffered, seeing that kind of trust made me feel better, and I wanted more."

She took a breath, but kept her eyes locked with his. "I'm ashamed to admit it, but I selfishly dismissed the conflict of interest because I knew no one would ever know if I took something for myself this one time."

He felt the sting of her confession like a slap. From the moment he laid eyes on her, he'd wanted her. Finding out he was a means to an end messed with his head more than it should.

"So, I was a hate-fuck to piss off your grandfather. But somehow your plan of never having to do business with me failed. Why are you the person here tonight and not some faceless suit from Devereaux Inc.?"

She reached out for the table as if to steady herself. Was this an act to get her out of the hot water she'd landed them both in? Or was this real?

"Are you okay?"

She closed her eyes and nodded, pointing to the chair beside her. When he nodded, she sat down, crossing one thick leg over the other as she leaned back.

He pulled out a chair, crowding in on her. Sure, he could stop being a jerk and give her some space. But this woman had purposely played with his damn career. He wasn't about to let her off the hook.

"When you're born into the Devereaux family, your place is pretty much decided from conception. My grandfather and my mother ran the company's legal department until my mother had me and decided motherhood was more important than corporate law. Being a stay-at-home mom and wife became her joy in life, and she never wanted to go back to practicing law. My grandfather idolizes her, and he's never gotten over the fact that she won't be around to take over at his retirement. Long story short, in his eyes, I don't measure up to the standard my mother set."

She tapped her fingers against her thigh, a move he was sure she did absentmindedly. But to him, it just brought back the memory of how good those elegant fingers felt against his naked flesh.

*Focus, Lennox.*

"My great-uncle is dying of cancer and had a major setback recently that landed him in the hospital. As his brother, my grandfather decided his place was at Uncle Ace's side. As a result, I'm now the interim head of legal. And when he dropped this deal in my lap, I couldn't tell him I had to step down because I'd compromised myself and the company by recklessly sleeping with the city councilman responsible for the permits we need."

He let his gaze slide down the length of her, trying to gain perspective. Her strength and power had called to him when they met. Which was why it bothered him so much that such a formidable person seemed so broken before him.

"Why doesn't your grandfather recognize your worth? Do you have a habit of making bad deals?"

She shook her head. "No, I'm focused. I know what I want, and I have no qualms about reaching beyond the limits others have placed on me. But to my grandfather, that looks like impulsive recklessness. If I were a man, he'd call me a trailblazer. If I were my mother, he'd call me brave. But because I'm neither of those things, he can only see me through his narrow perspective."

She leaned forward, placing a warm hand on top of his. "I'm sorry for putting you in a compromising position. It was never my intention. But I have to ask, where do we go from here?"

He switched the position of their hands so his now engulfed hers. He still couldn't help taking in the inviting warmth her touch brought. "Well, in my mind, how we proceed depends on how you answer my next question."

She narrowed her gaze as she leaned forward. "What's that?"

"Are you carrying my child?"

Her tongue felt heavy, so she swallowed to try to loosen it from the roof of her mouth. She tried to pull her hand out of his, but he held on tighter, forcing her to meet his determined gaze.

"I'm not pregnant, Lennox."

She searched his gaze for the relief she assumed would be there. Instead, she found a flicker of something sad and reserved in his eyes that puzzled her. Could he be disappointed?

"Are you sure? Did you take a test?"

She shook her head. "I didn't have to. My period arrived right on schedule."

He released her hand then, leaning back against his chair. His expression was inscrutable, but whatever he was thinking was weighing heavily on his mind if the distant look in his eyes was any indication.

"This isn't the best situation, Angel."

The way he'd comfortably slipped back into using her middle name, the name he'd called while he'd given her pleasure beyond her wildest dreams, made the skin at the nape of her neck tingle with excitement.

"I realize that, Lennox."

"No, you don't. It's not just a matter of impropriety. I'm in the middle of a campaign. Something like this gets out and my bid for mayor is over."

She nodded. He was right. This could destroy his career. And out of all the things she'd wanted from their one night together, him losing an election was never one of them.

"It was one night, Lennox. Neither of us should lose everything we've worked for because of it. I think if we can agree to keep things professional, we can both get what we want out of this deal."

He stood up, leaning against the large conference table as he looked down at her, making her feel consumed with a single glance.

"Could you so easily forget what we shared, how we were together?"

Her throat felt tight, and her body burned from within. Forget? No, she doubted she'd ever be able to wipe what they'd shared completely from her mind.

"As good as that night was, I can't let it negatively impact Devereaux Inc. I'll do whatever I have to, to make sure we both get what we want, Lennox."

Something flashed in his eyes. She couldn't tell if it was anger or acceptance. After several long moments of holding her gaze, he looked down at his polished shoes.

"The only problem is, we don't want the same thing,

Angel. You want to build new, expensive buildings that will displace so many of my constituents. I can't let that happen."

"So you're saying you're turning down my proposal without even reading it?"

"Oh," he answered quickly, "I've read it. It's impressive. But I can't sign off on it. You want gentrification, but the only thing I'm interested in is urban renewal. So, if you want those permits, you'll redesign your proposal to suit my desires."

She frowned. "You're splitting hairs. What's the difference between the two?"

"Clear your schedule for tomorrow and I'll show you the difference."

Intrigued by his suggestion, she stood, walking past him, plucking a paper plate from the stack on the other side of the table. She opened the pie he'd abandoned when she walked into his office and placed two large slices on her plate.

She took a bite of one, savoring the flavor and perfect texture of the well-done slice of pizza. Then she walked back to where he was leaning against the table, reached past him, picked up her bag and nodded. "I'll see you at noon."

She walked toward the door, only to be stopped by the liquid sound of his deep baritone. "I don't have your address to pick you up."

She didn't turn around. She grabbed the doorknob and smiled to herself. "I still have your number. I'll text it to you. See you tomorrow, Councilman."

"Oh," he called out before she could step through the

doorway. "Make sure to dress comfortably. Wouldn't want you ruining a perfectly good pair of Jimmy Choos."

She looked over her shoulder and had to tighten her grip on the doorknob to steel herself against his brazen, half-cocked grin. It was the same smile he'd worn when he exercised such knowing control over her body in that office at The Vault. She'd fallen prey to it then. But never again. Not when everything she ever wanted hung in the balance.

"No worries, Councilman. I'll be ready." She nodded one last time as the silent *for you* hung in the air. No matter how much she wanted to, she couldn't drop her guard. If she did, she knew he'd destroy her.

The only problem was she knew how beautiful and satisfying that destruction could be.

# Seven

Amara stood in front of the mirror turning this way and that, trying to figure out if her outfit was casual enough. She had an entire bedroom as a walk-in closet in her Clinton Hill brownstone, filled with designer clothes for every occasion. Elegant evening gowns made specifically to fit her deep curves, power suits to show people how formidable she was before she spoke a single word, and casual wear that often cost as much as the couture items in her possession. But after Lennox's comment about her Jimmy Choos, somehow everything she put on felt like too much.

He hadn't said anything that could be seen as an outright insult. But the smirk on his face coupled with the way the designer's name fell from his lips somehow gave her the impression that dressing up for him today would be out of place.

After changing several times, she finally settled on a pair of high-rise capri jeans, Stan Smith Adidas and a cute halter top. She piled her dark curls on top of her head in a pineapple, pulling a few tendrils out at her temples to cascade against her face. A simple pair of gold hoop earrings and a little Pat McGrath lip gloss completed her outfit.

"This is as casual as I know how to get, Councilman," she said to her reflection in the mirror. "Hopefully it meets your approval."

*Why do you care if it doesn't?*

She didn't have time to answer her own question before the doorbell rang. She grabbed her Louis Vuitton wristlet, popped her ID, credit card and lip gloss inside, and headed for the door.

"Right on time, Council—" She couldn't finish her sentence, the sight of him stopping all conscious thought and forcing her to focus on one thing: how absolutely fine this man was.

He wore a simple navy polo shirt that stretched tightly against his muscular chest and arms. His khaki shorts fell below his knees, displaying his strong tanned legs, sprinkled with fine dark hair.

"Were you peeking into my closet this morning, Angel? It seems we're matching."

She pulled her eyes away from a slow perusal of his body to meet his gaze, but still couldn't figure out what he was talking about.

"Our footwear. We're both wearing Stan Smiths. I wouldn't have thought a blue blood like yourself would know anything about these classics."

She blinked a few times, as she tried to force her brain/tongue connection to start working again.

"As you said," she finally began, stopping briefly to clear her throat, "they're classics. It doesn't matter what tax bracket you're in, some things are universal."

An awkward moment of silence passed between them as they just stared at each other in the doorway. She smiled, more to herself than him, thinking that this was more than an uncomfortable silence. They were both obviously checking each other out.

*So, it ain't just me. Good to know.*

"Shall we?" She made to leave but he tilted his head, then lifted his hands. He held a brown bag in one, and a drink tray with what appeared to be two cups of coffee in the other.

"I brought breakfast. We'll need the energy for what I have planned today. You mind if we eat here and then start our day together?"

How she'd managed to miss both the smell and sight of the food was beyond her. Because from the moment she'd opened the door, all she'd focused on was him, that's how.

"Sure," she managed to answer. "Follow me."

She led him through the large foyer, down the long hall to the kitchen in the back. She offered him one of the stools at the counter.

He sat down, pulling out what appeared to be sandwiches wrapped in foil. She hadn't been hungry, but the moment she peeled back the aluminum wrapping and the divine aroma of scrambled eggs, bacon and butter overwhelmed her senses, she was suddenly starving.

"This smells heavenly." She nearly sang those words. "Thank you, Lennox. This was very kind."

"Nothing like bacon, egg and cheese on a buttered roll from the bodega to start your day."

She picked up half of her sandwich, biting into it without any pretense. Fried breakfast food wasn't really her jam, but hell if this wasn't the best thing she'd ever tasted.

"My God, this is good."

"I take it you don't frequent the bodega on the corner much, do you?"

She couldn't bother with trying to speak. Instead, she shook her head as she chewed on her next delicious bite.

He kept a knowing smile on his face; it seemed that he was enjoying watching her eat. She went to pick up one of the cups of coffee to wash her food down, but there was something unpleasant about the smell that made her pull back.

"Is something wrong? There's cream and sugar in the bag if you want."

She replaced the cup and shook her head. "No, I usually take it black, but for some reason it doesn't seem all that appealing today. I've got apple juice in the fridge. Do you want some?"

"I'm good with water if you have it. If the coffee doesn't suit you, that's probably a hint I shouldn't be drinking it, either."

She nodded, turning around and quickly grabbing their beverages from her fully stocked fridge.

She handed him his bottle of water and twisted the top off her juice, taking a long drink from it. When she was done, he was still staring at her with a strange smirk on his face that she couldn't read.

"What?"

He shrugged, leaning forward on the counter. "Nothing. It's just, most of the people I spend time with are always so careful about appearances. I rarely get to see someone enjoying simple pleasures such as good food. A woman who will actually eat in front of me like a normal human being is a rarity in my professional circles. It's refreshing to watch."

She stood still, trying her best to decipher whether he was being honest or sarcastic. But then her gaze landed on the remaining half of her sandwich, and she figured her time was better spent enjoying her food than trying to decode the man sitting at her kitchen counter. She'd figure him out later. Right now, her sandwich was calling her name.

"So, tell me what you see."

She looked at him with a raised brow as she tried to figure out what he was getting at. They were standing on the corner of Gates and Clinton avenues, around the corner from her family's residence and business.

"I see Devereaux Manor right here. It's the jewel of the block. But when you turn the corner onto Gates Avenue, I see dilapidated buildings being torn down and rebuilt to match the splendor of Devereaux Manor. The new construction will bring a nicer-looking neighborhood and boost the local business district."

He nodded, but there was something in the depth of his gaze hidden that suggested he didn't share her perspective.

"Let me guess," she hedged. "You see something different?"

He turned around in a circle with his arm held out as if to put their surroundings on display for her.

"You're right." His tone was neutral without the tinge of judgment she'd expected. "We don't see the same thing."

He stepped in front of her again, meeting her gaze, forcing her to engage even though everything about his eyes warned her that retreat was her best bet.

"I see an area where kids used to play, where the old folks who carried the history of this neighborhood could sit and share their knowledge with the younger generations. Where you see business revitalization in all the new upscale stores popping up, I see places that are removing the personal element from shopping, replacing the traditional small businesses where merchants were also your neighbors. Like the bodega where I picked up breakfast. The owners have been part of this neighborhood for generations."

Lennox's comment seemed to suggest that she might live in Clinton Hill, but obviously she was missing something.

"I see a neighborhood where people could shop close to their homes for their necessities while paying reasonable prices for their goods," he continued. "Gentrification is robbing them of their ability to do that."

She tore her gaze away from his, trying to picture the oasis he was attempting to paint with his words. But to her, no matter how she tried, she couldn't see things through his eyes.

"There are so many specialty and boutique shops

whose merchandise come with a higher price point, it's impossible for the working class, let alone residents on fixed incomes, to acquire basic goods."

The gentle conviction in his voice pulled her gaze back to his, tethering her to him, making her think about what he was saying, and feeling the impact of his words, too.

"Where you see shiny new buildings, I see higher rents designed to draw in people in higher tax brackets while it forces the people who've lived here for generations out of their homes and the very neighborhood they helped build and sustain."

His words came down like a cartoon mallet on top of her head. But this was no cartoon. If she believed Lennox's perspective, she was bringing untold doom to Clinton Hill.

She took a deep breath as they continued their walk, trying to reconcile what Lennox was saying with the development plans she was tasked with executing for Devereaux Inc. She might not have grown up poor, but she loved Clinton Hill just as much as the next resident. Lennox seemed to be insinuating otherwise, and the more she thought about it, the more it angered her.

"I'm not trying to harm Clinton Hill. I resent how you're insinuating that I am. This project will bring millions of dollars in revenue to this neighborhood. And not just to the rich people. Everyone in Clinton Hill will benefit."

After a few more stops on their tour, they were back in front of her doorstep. The awkward silence they'd initially shared returned, but for wholly different reasons.

"Angel." He whispered her name, sending tingles

up her arms. Her entire life, she'd only heard her middle name spoken when one of her parents was calling her by her entire government name when she was in trouble. But the decadent sound of it on his lips made it feel like she never wanted to be addressed by any other name again.

"I wasn't insinuating you don't care about Clinton Hill. I just think your perspective is skewed because you've only ever experienced it as the heiress to a billion-dollar legacy."

She huffed, rolling her eyes. "You say that like it's a sin."

He shook his head, stepping closer to her, leaning against the iron safety railing on the stoop. "It's not a sin to be wealthy, Angel. I spent a lot of years in corporate law working myself out of poverty. Having money is really nice. I just want you to look at the total picture."

She held up a hand to stop him. "Lennox, even if I agreed with you, which I don't, it doesn't matter what my perspective is. As the head of legal at Devereaux Inc., my job is to get these permits from the city and get this project underway. I can't deviate from that objective."

He nodded, giving her a side glance and a half smile that highlighted the deep dimple in his cheek.

"What if there was a way for us to both get what we want? Would you be willing to think about the big picture then? We've both spent a lot of years negotiating. We know how this works. The best deals have compromise built into them. So, what do you say to me picking you up again so we can gather more intel to make this deal equitable?"

His words created small flutters in her stomach that bordered on uncomfortable. Agreeing to meet with him again was definitely the wrong move for Devereaux Inc. But she couldn't look away from that dimple, and found herself nodding against her better judgment.

"Good," he responded. "I'll call you with details."

He made his way down her steps and turned just before he reached the gate. "Oh, and Angel, I promise you won't regret this."

He gave her a playful wink and disappeared through the gate and down the block. And the only reply she could come up with was, "For both our sakes, I'd better not."

# Eight

"Is that my favorite son I hear coming through the door?"

Lennox stopped in his tracks the moment he heard his mother's greeting. Up until his father's death, the moment either he or his sister walked through the door, Della Carlisle had celebrated their arrival exactly the same way.

But since they'd lost his father, and his mother had lost the love of life, she'd barely done more than give him a cursory hello when he entered her home.

He walked down the hall of the two-family building he'd purchased for her and his baby sister when his father died. This purchase had been more than a financial investment. It had been a safeguard, a way to make sure someone was always around to keep an eye on his mother. As hard as she took his dad's death, he didn't trust that she'd be okay alone.

When he found her in the kitchen plating up food, he leaned down and kissed her lightly tanned cheek.

"How's my favorite girl doing today?"

"Better now that my baby boy is here to spend time with me."

He tilted his head, while trying to stifle the smile on his lips. "You know I'm the oldest of your two kids, right?"

"Doesn't matter." She dismissed him with a wave of her hand. "You're always going to be the baby boy they placed in my arms all those years ago."

He regarded her carefully. She sounded like the mother he'd adored before she'd lost the other half of herself. But he was so afraid to trust this newfound exuberance.

"So, what's with all this food. Looks like fried catfish and grits? You haven't cooked like this since..."

"I know," she responded softly, her pain palpable.

Determined not to spoil her mood, he quickly sat down, minding his manners and waiting until his mother said grace before he tucked into what he knew was going to be a fantastic meal.

He was halfway through his first piece of catfish before he could pull his gaze up from his plate.

"Mama, you put your foot in this. This catfish is so good."

"Glad you like it. I was inspired to make it."

"By what?" He brought his focus back to his plate, scooping up a spoonful of grits as she continued.

"I dreamed fish last night."

He momentarily forgot how to chew and swallow, causing the grits to skid a little too close to his airway and kicking in his gag reflex.

"You all right, baby?" his mom asked while he tried to get through his coughing fit. "Raise your arms up so you don't choke."

He wasn't all right. Not by any stretch of the imagination. Growing up, he'd always been told that dreaming fish meant someone was pregnant.

"Like I said, I dreamed fish," she continued. "And you know that means another baby is coming into this family. So, you got anything you want to tell me?"

His coughing finally quieted enough that he could speak. He could feel his brows knitting together as he looked her. "Me? What about my sister? She's the one that has a wife living upstairs with her."

His mama kept her gaze leveled at him. "I asked your sister. It ain't her."

"Well, it ain't me, either."

He grabbed his empty glass and filled it with iced tea from the nearby pitcher. He drank half the glass in one gulp, trying to get himself together.

"Layla and Mina have decided they're gonna wait a little longer to expand their family. So that leaves you."

It couldn't be. Angel had said she wasn't pregnant. There had to be some mistake. But as he remembered his mother's fish dreams had accurately predicted the last seventeen pregnancies in his very large extended family, panic settled in.

"Mama, I don't know what you're talking about. I'm not even seeing anyone."

"Well, somebody lyin', 'cause according to my dream, I'm sho' nuff about to be a grandmother."

The food he'd been enjoying a moment ago sat heavy in his stomach and he couldn't manage another bite. Instead, he stood from the table and went about washing the dishes as his mother finished her plate. When he was done, he hugged her, made excuses about work and headed straight for his car to make a call.

Two rings later, momentary relief bled through him as the call connected. "Hey, Lennox. What's go—"

"Angel, I need to see you immediately. Are you home?"

"Yeah."

"Don't go anywhere," he said with more force than he intended. "I'll be there in less than thirty minutes."

He ended the call with an abrupt tap of his thumb and started the ignition. Pulling out into traffic, he kept a repetitive litany on loop in his head.

*Please let my mama be wrong for once.*

A heavy, persistent knocking alerted Amara to Lennox's arrival. She rushed to the door, opening it wide to see Lennox midknock. The angular lines of his face were pulled tight, and his shoulders were high as if he was having difficulty breathing.

"Lennox, come in." He pushed past her, standing in the foyer looking back and forth as he tried to figure out which direction to go in. He didn't wait for her to guide him through the house; once he looked to the right and saw her living room, he stalked into it, pacing back and forth.

"Lennox, you're scaring me. What's wrong?"

He slid his hand over his bald head as he kept pacing. "Lennox, please."

He stopped, his panicked gaze latching on to hers, ratcheting up her concern.

"I think you're pregnant. And I need you to take a test to confirm it."

She stood there with her mouth open, shocked by both his words and his demand.

"Lennox, I've already told you I'm not pregnant and there's nothing for you to worry about."

"Yeah, except my mama dreamed fish, so I need you to be certain."

She stared at him, her eyes blinking rapidly as she tried to process what he was saying.

"Your mama dreamed fish? Did you really just burst into my house because of some superstitious wives' tale?"

He put his hands on his hips, confirming she'd jumped to the right conclusion. She was torn somewhere between being annoyed and falling into a fit of laughter. "I told you, I'm not pregnant. So, your mother's dream notwithstanding, you have nothing to worry about."

"You don't understand, Angel. My mother's fish dreams are never wrong. She never gets the interpretation, or the expecting parent, wrong. In this case, she's saying it's me. And since you're the only person I've had sex with recently, that means you're pregnant."

She didn't know if it was the conviction in his tone or the abject fear she saw in his wide hazel eyes. Whatever it was, she was beginning to get nervous.

"We need to go pick up a test right now."

She shook her head. "Lennox, you're a mayoral candidate and I'm a Devereaux. We can't just walk into Duane Reade and buy a pregnancy test. It would be all over the gossip rags before I could swipe my card at the register."

"Then what do you suggest?"

She walked over to him, grabbing his hand and leading him to a large sofa in the middle of the room. "I'll order one online and have it overnighted. By tomorrow I'll take it and put your mind at ease."

"You're assuming it's going to be negative. What happens if it isn't, Angel?"

The hell if she knew. Truly, she couldn't let herself think that far ahead. The timing of a pregnancy right now would complicate both their lives and careers in irrevocable ways. Ways she wasn't sure either of them was ready to face.

*How the hell did I get here?* As quickly as the question arose, her mind answered.

*Because you screwed a sexy man you know you had no business touching. The question you should be asking is what are you gonna do now.*

# Nine

The package arrived.

We'll know in the morning.

He'd waited for those texts all day. He was about to respond when he watched those maddening three dots appear on his screen, followed quickly by a new message.

Do you want to be here when I take it?

His thumb hovered over his phone, poised to respond. Of course, he wanted to be there. But after the way he'd barged into her house yesterday demanding she take a test, he wasn't sure she'd want him around. Honestly, it would serve him right if she didn't.

If you want me there, I want to be there.

Be here by six. Bring BEC sandwiches with you, please.

The price of entry?

Absolutely.

At least she was in good spirits. They were certainly going to need their senses of humor if the results came back the way he expected.

Amara smiled as she stood in her kitchen rereading her text conversation with Lennox. Even through text, she was reminded of what had attracted her to him in the first place.

*Aside from how fine he is, you mean?*

Well, his looks certainly hadn't been a problem that night at The Vault. But she'd been taken in by not just his appearance, but his presence.

As a confident woman who understood her power, it wasn't often she came across a man who was equally self-possessed, enough to not be threatened by her confidence. If memory served, Lennox had thrived off her strength that night.

*Amara, stop thinking about this man like that. This is serious.*

Serious was an understatement. According to Lennox, his mother's fish dreams were never wrong. Amara was aware of the mythical fish dream. She'd heard several variations of it from both the Black American and Afro-Latinx sides of her family. But there hadn't been a baby in their branch of the Devereaux clan since she was born. So, to her, this kind of thing was all superstition with very little evidence of actual truth. The idea that Lennox's mother could be right shook her to her core.

Could she even picture herself as a mother?

Financially of course, there was nothing stopping her from raising a child. But was this what she'd imagined for her life, especially at this stage of her career now?

She was finally getting everything she wanted. Her grandfather was handing her the reins. And as much as they'd discussed contracts and negotiations, she couldn't recall if he'd ever expressed his views on single motherhood. Would they be old-fashioned? Would he think her irresponsible for having a baby out of wedlock? Would that be enough to make him change his mind about promoting her?

Four weeks had passed since she'd been with Lennox. Other than miraculously being cured of her normal addiction to coffee, a fact she'd attributed to her dropping into bed by nine every night for the last two weeks, she had no symptoms whatsoever. No nausea, no cravings, and most importantly, her period had come right on schedule.

Or had it?

She scoured her brain, trying to recall some random piece of information from her high school health ed classes.

"Implantation bleeding?"

A cold chill spread through her as she thought of her last health ed teacher explaining it. *It's bleeding that occurs at the beginning of pregnancy caused by*

*the embryo implanting itself into the womb. Sometimes*
*pregnant women mistake it for their period.*

"No. It couldn't be."

She continued to muse until she heard the doorbell
ring. With the nerves in her stomach beginning an in-
convenient two-step, she opened the door to find Lennox standing there holding up a familiar brown bag with
large grease spots on it. More than expensive gems or
designer clothes, she couldn't remember ever being so
excited by a visitor's gift.

"Price of passage." Lennox smiled as he waved the
bag back and forth in front of her. "Since you seemed
to like the first so much, I got you an extra one for later
if you want it."

She snatched the bag and opened it, taking a long
sniff of the glorious aroma. "I could kiss you."

He chuckled as she stepped aside and let him in.
"Kissing me is what got us into trouble in the first
place."

He wasn't wrong. That kiss had set her ablaze. Any
thoughts she'd had about restraint went out the window
once her lips touched his.

"I was about to say something slick." She shrugged.
"But it would be a lie. It was a pretty great kiss."

He chuckled, nodding in agreement, then clapped
his hands together as they stood facing each other in
the foyer.

"So, do you wanna eat first or take the test?"

Smiling as she watched him, she could tell by the
way his hands were shoved in his pockets and he was
shifting his weight from one foot to the other that he
was anxious.

"Come on. Let's put you out of your misery. I'll take the test now and we can eat later."

She headed for the stairs and motioned for him to follow her. They'd already slept together; him being in her bedroom was no big deal at this point. She directed him to the bench at the foot of her king-size bed. She stood there, looking into his eyes, wondering how the next few minutes could alter the course of both their lives.

"Angel." He took her hand and gently ran thumb across her knuckles. "No matter what that test says, I'm here. You're not alone in this."

Used to doing everything for herself, the idea of having someone to hold her hand as she ventured into unfamiliar territory was a comfort she didn't know she needed.

She nodded and closed her eyes, needing to break the connection. She'd seen this man partially naked and had shared her body with him. Yet somehow, this moment was so much more intimate. And standing there as Lennox's gaze reached beyond her defenses made her feel vulnerable in a way that wasn't necessarily comfortable for someone who prided herself on being a corporate conqueror.

He released her hand and she headed into the en suite bathroom. The test was sitting on her double vanity looking like a ticking bomb that had the possibility of blowing her career to tiny bits. She picked it up carefully, her fingers gingerly caressing the sides as she tried to steel her nerves.

*No sense in dragging this out, girl. Pee on the stick and find out for certain if you'll be a mother or not.*

\* \* \*

Lennox sat on the bench, leaning over with his forearms on his knees, praying that for once, his mother's dreams were just superstition and not premonition.

He wasn't afraid of having children. He'd always imagined he would become a father and pass down the things his parents had shared with him to a child of his own. But the timing, and his precarious connection to Angel, made things complicated in ways he wasn't prepared to deal with. Most notably, for his mayoral candidacy.

The door to the en suite opened and Angel reentered the bedroom. He locked gazes with her, his brows lifting in expectation of an answer.

"It's still processing." The test sat atop a paper towel in the palm of her hand. "I'm too anxious to watch this little digital timer tick by myself, so I thought I'd make you suffer with me."

She shared a shaky half smile with him that made his heart constrict inside his chest. He'd known from the moment he'd laid eyes on her that she was fierce and capable. But right now, she was anxious, and protective instincts he didn't know he possessed started flaring up.

He opened his arms to her and waited until she finally laid down her armor and sat down next to him, sliding into his embrace.

"Are you afraid?" When she didn't respond he smiled. "It's okay if you are. I certainly am."

"Let me guess," she replied. "Knocking up a one-night stand you never had any intention of seeing again wasn't on your bucket list?"

He chuckled at how she used sarcasm to deflect emo-

tion and filed that bit of information away in his things-
I'm-learning-about-Angel file.

"Getting you pregnant may not have been on my
agenda, but I'd be lying if I said I didn't want to see you
again after the night we shared."

"Really?" Her reply grated on his nerves a bit and
he couldn't tell why. He didn't make a habit of following up with one-night stands. But for some reason, he
didn't like the implication of her question when applied
to the night they'd spent together.

"Are you saying I was so easily forgettable for you?"

"A powerful man needing his ego stroked. Who
would've thought it?"

"You're deflecting, Counselor. Answer the question."

She paused a moment, but he could feel her mouth
curving into a smile against his chest.

"I might've had a thought or two about you before I
walked into your office."

"Well, depending on what that stick you're holding
says, we might be spending much more time together
than either of us ever anticipated." He placed a gentle
kiss atop her head and cupped her cheek with his hand
as they sat there quietly for the next few minutes, waiting to discover their fate.

Her watch buzzed, making her stiffen against him.
He loosened his hold on her, but slid his hand down her
arm and interlaced their fingers. She looked up at him
and steadied herself with an audible breath before she
opened her palm and turned the pregnancy test wand
over to view the digital screen.

Right there in bold digital print, one word confirmed
what he'd known since his mother had informed him of

her dream. Angel, a woman he hardly knew, a woman currently seeking to do business with his office, was pregnant with his child.

He felt her stiffen in his arms and it made him tighten his hold on her. Whatever was going through her head he needed her to know he was her anchor.

"Tell me what you're thinking, Angel."

She turned to him, blinking just before her tears spilled down her cheeks. "I… My thoughts are all over the place. I'm terrified."

Yeah, he was scared out of his goddamn mind, too. But there, mixed in with the fear, was something else, something bright, uplifting and unexpected. But that didn't mean Angel was feeling that, too.

"Is that all you feel? Fear?"

She gave him a shaky smile as she shook her head. "If you're asking what I think you are, however we created this child, I'm not considering terminating the pregnancy."

He squeezed her tighter. "Thank you for sharing that with me. And for the record, whatever your decision, I would've supported you."

Quiet cloaked the room as they both tried to get their emotional footing.

"Is it weird that despite our situation, I'm happy, too?" she finally asked.

Lennox felt his smile growing wider. His campaign manager was going to have a fit once Lennox shared this news. But he didn't care. He was gonna be a father and nothing else seemed to matter in that moment.

"We're having a baby, Angel."

She sighed, closing her eyes and leaning into him.

"We're having a baby, Lennox. What are we going to do?"

Her question stoked his apprehension again. The hell if he knew what the next steps were. The sound of his heart beating so loudly beneath his ribs made it difficult for him to think anything other than, *Oh shit. Oh shit. Oh shit*, on a repetitive loop. He closed his eyes, blocking everything else out, and then the solution came to him.

He turned to her, squeezing her hand to get her attention. She asked him again. "What are we going to do, Lennox?"

And with a wobbly smile of his own he said, "We get married."

# Ten

"Hell no."

She spoke the words as easily as her own name. Probably a little too harshly, from the way Lennox recoiled in response.

"Angel, we have to."

"Actually, no, we don't. We don't know anything about each other, Lennox. We can't get married. Why would we?"

"Angel, we're having a baby."

She stood up, pacing back and forth to help her think. What the hell was he thinking? "Yes, I'm aware. But this isn't some 1950s drama. I don't need a husband to have a child and maintain my respectability. I don't give a damn about what anyone else thinks. And in case you haven't noticed, I'm a Devereaux. I'm more than capable of taking care of a child financially."

"Personally, I don't care what people think, either. But professionally, this could be career suicide. I have to think about that. As for your identity I'm well aware of who you are...*now*." His eyes narrowed into two tiny accusing slits as he leveled his gaze at her.

"So this is my fault?"

He tilted his head slightly. "That we created a baby? No, we both bear that responsibility. That I slept with you in the first place? Yeah, that's your fault. You knew who the hell I was and how problematic things would get if we found ourselves in a situation. I wasn't given the same courtesy of knowing your identity. If I'd been aware, there's no way in hell we'd be here now."

The cold glint in his eyes made her shiver. "Lennox, I've already explained..."

"That you were in a bad way and exercised poor judgment, and that you had no intention of ever seeing me again. Yeah, I got that part. But that's not how life has worked out. I'm campaigning in the primary to be the next mayor of New York City. The incumbent is a man who keeps pointing out that I'm unmarried, suggesting that I have no ties to ground me, making me too flighty and unsettled to get the job done."

Lennox stood with his legs wide and his arms folded against his chest, making a sexy yet imposing picture. "Up until now, constituents haven't bought into his BS. But the moment it gets out I'm having a baby with someone my office might end up doing business with, my bid for mayor is over. You withheld information that kept me from making an informed decision. You were wrong and you owe me. You're going to marry me."

Unbothered, Amara put her hands on her hips and

jutted one out. Two could play this "I shall not be moved" game.

"I'm *going* to marry you?" she spat, slightly amused but mostly pissed off by his edict. "Last I checked, marriage was a voluntary agreement. You don't have enough leverage over me to make me pour you a glass of water, let alone marry you."

Something hard and dangerous sparked in his eyes as he stepped closer into her personal space.

"I wonder what David Devereaux would have to say about that?"

The mention of her grandfather's name made an internal tremor quake throughout her body.

"If I remember correctly, when we met, you were upset because your boss was giving you grief about being too reckless at work. Sounds to me like he wouldn't be too thrilled if he knew how we ended up here."

She folded her arms across her chest. "That sounds like you're threatening me."

"Call it whatever you like. But if you don't agree to marry me immediately, I'm going directly to David and telling him about the unethical game his granddaughter played and how it's going to cost me a campaign and Devereaux Inc. millions, because there's no way I can give permits to a company with such an unprincipled leader."

He took one step closer, closing the last sliver of distance between them. "I wonder how quickly the old man would end his temporary leave and snatch control away from you if he knew all that."

She could feel her throat tightening as she tried to

swallow and tamp down both her anger and fear. Amara had no doubt her grandfather would end her trial period as head counsel in a heartbeat.

"What happened to all that smooth talking about you being here for me, Lennox? You've strangely gone from comforting me to blackmailing me. How's that work?"

"I *am* here for you." His words were softer but still managed to hold a sharp, frigid quality that put her on the defensive. "I want to be here for you. But I need the same kind of support from you. Neither of us need lose our careers over this. Marrying protects us both."

"I see how it protects you." This situation was definitely more advantageous for him with respect to his career. But there were too many variables where hers was concerned. "How does this protect my job? Are you saying you'll give me the permits if I marry you?"

His brow furrowed, registering mild shock. "I would never promise you something like that. Us having a child together is conflict of interest enough. When we marry, I'll have my assistant set up a third-party panel who will handle the entire process. Whatever they decide will be final. So even if the outcome doesn't go your way, you'll have to abide by it."

She shook her head. "That's not fair, Lennox. This marriage would give you exactly what you want by protecting your career. Why would I agree to something that doesn't provide me the same assurances?"

"Again," he responded, his smooth features schooled into an inscrutable expression, "perhaps you should've thought of that when you slept with me under false pretenses. I didn't get the chance to make a choice about putting my career on the line by sleeping with you.

Seems fitting the tables are turned now. Don't you think?"

*He's got you there, girl.*

Fire bubbled inside of her. He was right, of course. But that didn't mean she had to like the fact that he had no qualms about putting her in her place so succinctly.

She dropped her gaze, trying to find a moment of reprieve from the intensity of his. "But we don't love each other, Lennox. Hell, I'm not even sure if I like you all that much. How's a marriage going to work between us? We're going to make each other miserable."

He lifted her chin, locking eyes with her again. "We knew enough about one another to create this child. The rest will work itself out."

She stepped back, trying her best to put distance between them to keep her thoughts clear. When he was this close, touching her even in the most benign way, her brain shut off and her body completely took control.

"I'll ask you again, what about love, Lennox? I come from a family where marriage is sacred. Love is our bedrock. We'd be making a mockery of that."

"I'm not looking for love, Angel. My parents adored each other so much that when my father died, my mother became a broken shell. She gave up on life and just sat back waiting for death to claim her so she could be reunited with my dad. That sounds romantic, but it's the most painful thing I've ever lived through. I won't allow that to happen to me."

He pulled his hand down over his face and took a steadying breath. Although the hard exterior was still there, she could see tiny cracks in his resolve that made her ache for him.

"I can offer you companionship, partnership and kindness. I can't offer you love."

The hard glint in his eyes didn't make her afraid. Sadness, that's what she felt clawing at her as she watched him. She knew they didn't love each other. They'd just met. But the fact that he couldn't even be open to the possibility made her sad that her child would never know the joy of growing up with parents who adored each other like she had.

"If love is off the table, what are your terms?"

He seemed to relax, his shoulders dropping slightly as he prepared to answer her. "One, we stay married for as long as I'm in office. Two, we reside in the same household. Three, whenever we're in public, we play the role of devoted spouses and parents. Four, as long as we're married, there will be no outside relationships. We're faithful for however long we're tied to each other."

She could feel her forehead pinching into a sharp point. "You could end up being in office for eight years. What are we supposed to do about sex?"

He quickly threaded his fingers through her hair and seared her lips with a kiss. Her mouth burned from his touch, and when she moaned, trying her best to deepen the kiss, he tore his mouth away from hers and stared down at her. "If we need sex, we come to each other. It doesn't matter to me how this marriage came about. If I take you as my wife, you're mine, Angel. No one else touches you besides me. I won't be made a fool of by anyone, least of all a cheating wife."

Amara didn't scare easily. But the harsh tone of his voice had her wondering if for once she'd bitten off more than she could chew. Because the way he'd said the word *mine* made her afraid and more than a little aroused. Either way, she realized things were getting out of hand.

Especially when his fingers tightened in her hair, and he pulled her against the hard planes of his body. She'd never been a woman who cared much about hard pecs and abs. But there was something about the firm foundation of Lennox's body that felt like hallowed ground to her. And as he wrapped his arm around her waist, locking in their position, she noticed instantly that his pecs and abs weren't the only part of his body that was hard, a fact she was most grateful for at the moment.

Much like the first and only time they were together, her clothes seemed to somehow fall away of their own accord, and she was pressed against hot flesh, her arms instinctively wrapping around him, determined to hold on.

Lennox must have somehow read her mind, understood that her need to be closer to him was much more than simple attraction. It was desperation. Like dehydrated ground soaking up rain, she savored every kiss, every touch until he hoisted her up, carrying her to her bed and lowering her to the mattress.

She quickly realized she wasn't the only person desperate for their bodies to connect. As she lay back on locked elbows, she watched him rip his clothing from his body, until he was naked in all his beautiful glory. Even though she knew he was a threat to everything she was trying to protect, she didn't run away, didn't put up the slightest bit of fight. She wanted this, and she couldn't see past the haze of her desire long enough to care about how this was going to wreck her life later.

He covered her body with his, satisfying her need to touch him and be touched by him. But it wasn't enough. Even with his lips on hers, on the curve of her neck and shoulder, her collarbone, and then slowly moving down the line of her décolletage, she ached until his mouth finally met the turgid peak of one nipple while his fingers continued to travel down her abdomen, between her legs, until they were slipping through her wet folds.

"Damn, I've barely touched you and you're already dripping." He pulled his fingers to his mouth, licking the evidence of her arousal away before leaning down and kissing her, demanding she open for him, letting her taste herself on him.

All she could do was surrender because it was the most potent and enticing thing she'd ever experienced. When he pulled away slightly, still brandishing that wicked smile of his, she burned from the hold he had on her. She secretly reprimanded herself for the lack of dignity she was displaying.

She narrowed her gaze, frustrated by his obvious gloating as well as the delayed action.

"Don't flatter yourself." She managed to find enough air in her lungs to speak quickly. "Increased sexual desire is a symptom of pregnancy."

A wicked gleam in his eye now accompanied his exasperating smile.

"If that's what you need to tell yourself to help you sleep at night."

She was busted. She knew it and so did he. Which was the problem with this thing between them. Amara wasn't used to being at a tactical disadvantage. When it came to Lennox, she always seemed to find herself at his mercy, and that just wouldn't stand.

"Shut up and fuck me."

His eyes slightly widened, and she realized she'd caught him off guard. Before he could recover the upper hand, she locked her knees around him, flipping the two of them over so that she was on top and in control.

She leaned down, grabbing a foil packet from her nightstand. "Until we're comfortable foregoing them."

Just because she was pregnant didn't mean either of them was ready for unprotected sex. Without delay, she wrapped her hand around his girth. Stroking him up and down, letting her thumb caress the tip, thoroughly enjoying the full-body shudder he exhibited, she sheathed him in the condom. She grinned, reveling in the fact that she wasn't the only one affected by their explosive need.

She slowly lowered herself onto him, satisfied moans escaping them both with each inch she took into her body. The stretch was significant, but so titillating she had to fight with herself not to rush this process.

Soon she was seated, so full of him she could hardly tell where she ended and he began. She kissed him as she swiveled her hips, drawing the movement out, delighted by the almost painful grip he had on her hips as he tried to make her speed up her movements.

She refused to be rushed. This was too good, and she would enjoy it for as long as she could. When they weren't in bed, she spent too much energy trying to get the upper hand in a situation that was quickly getting out of control. But here, with her body clenched around his like they were molded to fit perfectly together, nothing else mattered. Not her job or her fear of losing the promotion she'd earned. Not the fact that her life was about to change irrevocably. And certainly not the fact that marrying Lennox was a bad idea, considering they barely knew each other.

She didn't have to think about any of that, as she swerved her hips then sat up so that she could experience the decadent pleasure of sliding up and down his length with her muscles clenching so tightly she could feel the erratic rhythm of his pulse. All she had to do was savor how good he felt inside her body as she climbed higher and higher, toward the climax that seemed just out of her reach.

He must have somehow realized her struggle, or maybe he was going through a similar one of his own. He sat up, wrapping one arm around her waist while the other hand went to the back of her neck.

In one fluid motion, she was on her back with one leg over his shoulder as he lodged himself as deeply as he could. He leaned forward, deepening his stroke, his cock sliding in at just the right angle to touch that elusive spot that would give her the release she was begging for.

"Please," she muttered, not giving a sliver of a damn at how needy and desperate she sounded. With one side of his mouth lifted in a grin, he placed a soft kiss on her calf before glancing down at her.

"Please what?" He ramped down his pace, swiveling his hips as slowly as she had, returning the torture she'd so happily doled out to him.

She was too close to tell him off. No way was she

doing anything that would make him deny her what her entire being was aching for.

"Please fuck me, Lennox." Her voice was a whispered cry that was equal parts pitiful and frustrated. "I need…"

"You need me." His voice was steady and forceful. It was a declarative statement, as if he knew this was an undisputed fact. "Say it," he commanded in a low growl. "Say you need me."

And there in that moment, when they battled like titans over whose will would reign supreme, her need grabbed hold of her so strongly, she knew he was the decided winner of this round.

"I need you, Lennox. Please."

She waited for the gloating, the bragging rights her concession handed him. But instead, there was relief in his eyes. He lowered her leg, leaning forward, burying his face in her neck as he whispered, "I need you, too. Can't do this without you."

Those words broke the dam holding back the wave of her climax. Like a tsunami crashing over her head, the powerful undercurrent of her orgasm dragged her beneath the rough waters of pleasure as he plowed into her with deep, strong strokes until she finally stopped struggling, and went willingly into the depths of satisfaction.

And when she thought she'd drown alone, every muscle in his body clenched as he joined her in bliss.

As they swam back to reality, their breathing labored and their chests heaving, he fell onto his side, grabbing her and pulling her into his embrace.

"Do you still have questions about what we'll do if either of us needs sex?"

Doubts? No. At this moment, all she had were guarantees. And the biggest one ran through her mind as her gaze met his. *This man is going to dismantle your entire life.* And as she watched a smile creep onto his face, all she could think was: *And you're going to let him.*

"Fine," she whispered. "I'll marry you."

# Eleven

Amara stood behind the railing and looked out over the ocean view balcony. Two days ago, Lennox had texted her travel information for an impromptu trip to Port Antonio, Jamaica. He'd taken care of all the arrangements, and as soon as she entered the property, she'd been whisked away to a beautiful private villa that boasted clean lines, minimal furnishings and open space.

Once the bellhop had escorted her to her room and left her bags lined up neatly in front of the wide closet doors, she headed straight for the patio. Marveling at the deep blue water, white sand and verdant greenery, Amara instantly felt her apprehension bleed away. She'd been on edge ever since Lennox told her they were flying down to Jamaica to elope.

A knock on the door pulled her from her musings.

She traversed the large bedroom and living area quickly, looking through the peephole to see a warped image of Lennox standing on the front porch.

She opened the door, stepping aside and letting him in.

"Glad to see you made it here safely." His tone was reserved. She led him to the living area and sat down next to him on the love seat.

"How was your flight?"

She wasn't sure how to answer that question. The pilot had gotten her to Jamaica safely, but flying alone on a private jet meant she'd had roughly four hours to dwell on how out of order things were.

"Angel?"

"My trip was thankfully uneventful." He raised his brow, encouraging her to continue. "The attendant mentioned how the last time I took the jet to the Caribbean, my parents were with me." He remained quiet, waiting for her to continue when she was ready.

"My parents and I are very close. We take impromptu family vacations all the time. The attendant just made me start thinking about how I'm going to explain all of this to them. They'll be thrilled to know they're going to be grandparents. But I think it's going to hurt them when they find out I married without their knowledge."

"And that's making you feel guilty?"

Guilt didn't really describe it. More than anything, she felt disappointment in herself for robbing them of sharing in this moment.

"During the father-daughter dance at my quinceañera, my dad told me how proud he was of the woman I was becoming and how the next father-daughter dance we had would be at my wedding."

Amara had never been an overly sentimental person. But knowing how much her father had looked forward to this and how she was intentionally taking it away from him weighed on her conscience more than she'd imagined.

"It seems that my moment of selfishness—that's how you put it, right?—is negatively impacting more than just you. This might be a pattern. You sure you want to go through with this wedding plan of yours?"

"This wedding is happening tomorrow evening, Angel." His words were direct, but she could see a brief flash of empathy in his eyes.

"Are you close to your parents?"

"Very," he responded, shifting on the sofa as if he needed to get comfortable before he could speak. "My dad passed away a few years ago. He was my best friend. My mom is thankfully still with us. She's this tiny little spitfire who still manages to get my younger sister and me to do exactly what she wants. Even my sister-in-law is wrapped around her finger."

"How do you think your mother's gonna feel about all of this?"

"She'll be pissed," he replied. "But I hope telling her about the baby will keep me from getting disowned."

There was an awkward pause. She presumed he was thinking about the consequences of their plan, too.

She looked around the room. "Thank you for the beautiful accommodations. Please send me the bill and I'll have you reimbursed."

His features tightened and she wondered what about her statement offended him.

"Angel." His acrid tone made her stiffen. "I may not be as rich as the Devereauxs, but after spending fifteen years as one of New York's top-paid corporate lawyers, I think I can afford to pay for a nice trip here and there without going broke."

"I didn't mean any offense, Lennox." Her apology was quick and true. "It would never dawn on me that a man I'm not really with would go through so much trouble for me."

He stretched his arm against the back of the love seat and leaned a little closer. "Angel, that's where you're wrong. We are together." He reached down and pulled her hand into his, resting both against his thigh. "Our union is definitely unorthodox. I'll give you that. But even though there's an expiration date on this marriage, I promise you, I intend to honor my vows to you for the duration. I hope I can count on you for the same."

Suddenly overwhelmed by emotion, she nodded in response, pulling a genuine smile from him.

"Good. Because I see no reason for us to hurt each other and be unhappy while we're together. So, get used to me doing nice things for you." He slid his hand to her stomach and splayed his fingers wide. "You're carrying my child. For that reason alone, I'll see to it you never want for anything."

Part of her delighted at his nurturing instincts. But another part wished that he wanted to spoil her for no other reason than she deserved it.

"Everything all right?"

"It's fine. Thank you for your generosity. I promise I'll make sure to enjoy our time here."

"Good," he replied. "I'm glad you're seeing things my way. Because first thing tomorrow morning, a masseuse, a hairstylist, a makeup artist, a nail technician and a personal stylist will be here to pamper and dress you, so you'll be the most beautiful bride to ever step on sand."

He placed a gentle kiss on her lips and granted her a kind smile as he pulled back. Before she could figure out what he was doing, he kneeled down in front of her, reaching into his pocket and retrieving a small velvet box.

"As I said, our union may not be conventional. But that doesn't mean it has to be any less significant. For as long as you choose to be my wife, I'll honor you, Angel. And that means if we're going to do this, we're going to do it right."

He opened the box, revealing a very large princess cut diamond with smaller round diamonds and rubies alternating on the band. She was about to say this was way too much for a fake marriage, but once she saw the ring sparkle, the words never came.

"Amara Angel Devereaux-Rodriguez. Will you do me the honor of meeting me on the beach tomorrow evening and becoming my wife?"

Excitement mixed with something unfamiliar spread through her until tears were spilling from her eyes. It had to be this pregnancy, because she couldn't remember being so easily brought to tears before in her life.

"Yes, Lennox."

That was as much as she got out before he slipped

the ring on her finger and brought his lips to hers. And as she lost herself in the high of his kiss, she pushed the fear trying to remind her that this wasn't real to the back of her mind. It wasn't smart. But this moment was too perfect to allow reality to intrude.

He broke the kiss, smiling as he stood. "I'll see you tomorrow on the beach. I'll be the guy standing next to the minister staring at you in awe."

He turned toward the door to leave, and she called his name. "Where are you going?"

"I have a room at the main hotel." He stared directly at her, his intense gaze making her feel like she should brace herself for whatever he was about to say next. "I didn't know if you'd be comfortable with me staying here with you."

This was the same man who'd threatened to expose her poor judgment to her grandfather unless she agreed to marry him. If she hadn't seen the concern in the depths of his brown eyes, she'd question how her comfort could matter to him at all.

"Angel." He turned to her, his features softening as he spoke. "Even when I push you to consider the greater good, that doesn't mean I don't care about what happens to you. Although I expect us to share a residence when we return home, you don't have to worry about me making other demands because we're married. Whether this is a marriage in name only is solely up to you."

A nervous bubble of laughter slipped past her lips. "I'd say the horse is already out of the barn on that one. Besides, didn't you just say we *are* together?"

"Yes, I did." He offered a casual shrug before tilting his head. "This is a partnership. An unconventional one, but still a partnership. I won't lie and say I don't want to share your bed, Angel. The two of us together are like fire and gasoline. I don't think there will ever be a time when I don't want to touch you." His eyes narrowed into slits, and she could feel the heat radiating from his intense gaze in the core of her chest. "But us being together doesn't mean I automatically have free range of your body. If you want more, you'll have to say so."

Those words were a challenge. A challenge she should ignore. This situation was messy enough. Him giving her an out on the physical intimacy was a boon she should gratefully accept. But she had never been known for letting things be, so she saw no reason to start now.

She stood up, folding her arms over her chest as she met his gaze. "All of this sounds really good, Lennox. But forgive me if I'm having a hard time buying it. Weren't you the same man who told me one of the rules of this marriage is if we want sex, we have to come to each other?"

He stepped in front of her, closing the space between them.

"I won't presume I'm owed sex because we're married, Angel. But for as long as this marriage lasts, I am the only person you will have sex with and vice versa. That is not up for negotiation. Do you understand me?"

Part of her wanted to curse him out for the ultimatum he was throwing down. He had no right to demand anything from her. But the tight set of his lips and the look in his eyes made her rethink the smart-ass comment hanging from the tip of her tongue. For the first time, Amara realized something about Lennox that made fear trickle down her spine. In this gorgeous, powerful man, she just may have met her match.

She swallowed, taking a step back before she nodded. "Understood."

# Twelve

Amara lay on the left side of the large empty bed with her eyes closed, hoping that if she remained still, she could stop the minutes from ticking and avoid the fate that awaited her later this evening. She turned over onto her back, pulling a smooth breath into her lungs. Lennox wasn't a monster. His actions last night proved it. He'd brought her to this island paradise, pledged his fidelity to her, and comforted her when she admitted her misgivings about marrying without her parents by her side.

But somehow, all his goodwill made this day even more difficult. It felt good. Too good. Good enough that she had to keep reminding herself this was fake, all a part of the show they were putting on. Getting caught up would be the worst thing she could do.

Realizing she couldn't hide from life or Lennox, she dragged herself out of bed and headed for the shower. Slightly soothed by the powerful spray of hot water against her skin, she quickly toweled off, grabbing the satin robe she'd placed in the bathroom last night before stepping in front of the large double vanity in the middle of the room.

Amara wiped the condensation from the foggy mirror as she stood trying her best to recognize the reflection staring at her.

"How did you end up in this mess, girl?"

She waited for her reflection to answer her, to in some way make it make sense to Amara. But somehow, the woman in the mirror remained silent, refusing to answer her question.

She looked down at the large engagement ring Lennox had placed on her finger last night. It was impressive, even by Devereaux standards. And that proposal, goodness, even knowing their union was a sham, she was moved by his declarations.

Amara heard a knock. Tightening the belt on her satin robe, she headed toward the door. Lennox had said her glam squad would show up early. However, she'd thought she'd at least have a chance to have breakfast before they arrived.

"Wow, I must need more work than I thought if you're here this early." She opened the door, ready to greet the people who would make her wedding-ready. But instead of a team of strangers holding garment bags and makeup trunks, she found Lennox standing in front of the door with her parents.

"Surprise!" Her mother and father yelled as they

surrounded her, hugging and kissing her. Stunned into silence, she looked up at Lennox to find a conspiratorial grin on his face.

*Why would he do this?*

He must have understood her unspoken question, because he waited for them to move farther into the villa before he addressed it.

"I know we said we wanted an intimate ceremony. But knowing how close we both are to our parents, I didn't feel right about going through with it without telling them."

Once her parents stepped aside, she opened her mouth to speak, but he held up a hand, interrupting her. "I hope you're not too upset with me. I just wanted to make this day as perfect for you as I could."

Quite frankly, she was so overwhelmed by the sight of her parents, she didn't know how to define her emotions. She was shocked, for certain, and probably more than a little ticked off he'd done this without her knowledge. This wasn't a regular wedding. Throwing her parents into the mix could have uncontrollable effects on this whole charade.

But deep in his eyes, there was something soft and comforting that brooked her anger and made her feel all warm and emotional. She'd like to blame it on pregnancy hormones, but the truth was she didn't know if this was a result of pregnancy or if this was just Lennox's power over her.

*"Mi amor,"* her father said softly to her mother. "Do you see this? I may have had my reservations when a total stranger called us and told us he was marrying

our daughter. But only someone who loves her terribly would do something like this for her."

Amara dropped her eyes, too ashamed to meet her father's gaze, and slightly afraid he'd see through their lies.

"Mr. Rodriguez, as I mentioned, I take full responsibility for waiting until the last minute to notify you. I was wrong for making plans that didn't include our families. I just hope you won't hold it against me and will give me the chance to prove my worth as Angel's husband."

"Angel?" her father repeated with a gentle smile on his face as he walked toward Lennox. "That's what you call my daughter, Angel?"

"Yes, sir," Lennox answered. "That's what she is to me."

Right there, she watched her father melt and fall in love with a man she was only tied to by convenience. And Amara knew her mother wouldn't be far behind from the way she was quietly dabbing her eyes.

They went out to the patio where a breakfast feast had been laid out. It took up most of the table.

"I assume this is more of your doing?" She smiled as Lennox shrugged, taking his seat next to her, directly across from her parents.

"It's our wedding day. Keeping a smile on your face is literally the one job I have."

"And you're very good at that job," her mother added. "From the look on my daughter's face now. Tell me, how'd you get so good at that?" She leaned forward, raising a brow. Her voice might have been liquid sunshine, but Amara recognized this look for what it was.

It was the precursor to the inquisition that always followed. "Obviously you haven't been seeing my daughter long, otherwise we'd have known about you. So how does a man I'm just meeting today get so adept at making my only child this happy?"

"Mamí…" Amara attempted to stop her mother's line of questioning when she felt strong but gentle fingers slide down her arm.

"It's fine, Angel. If I were in your parents' shoes, I'd have questions, too." She watched Lennox carefully, sitting back against her chair and hoping he knew what the hell he was doing.

"Your daughter and I met a little over a month ago at The Vault. The plain truth is, I couldn't take my eyes off her from the moment I saw her. Once we spoke, and bonded over what it's like to be young, Black and gifted, I couldn't let her go."

*Okay, Lennox. Score one for the Nina Simone reference. My mama will eat that up.*

Her mother nodded and sat back in her chair, taking a sip of water from her glass. "Attractive, generous, smart enough to recognize gold when he sees it, and cultured? You seem almost too good to be true, Lennox. Or are you simply giving me campaign face right now?"

Amara waited for Lennox to flinch. But he didn't so much as bat an eyelash. Instead, he spread his arm across the back of Amara's chair as he leaned closer to her.

"Mrs. Devereaux-Rodriguez, I'm the same whether I'm on the campaign trail or not. I'm all about protecting and supporting my people, working hard to see them thrive." He looked at Amara, and the fire sparking in the depth of his eyes pulled her in, tricking her senses into believing this could be real, if only for this moment. "That's even more true when it comes to my future bride and..."

He stopped short, tilting his head to silently ask her if he should continue. She couldn't help herself: she smiled, momentarily forgetting about how this situation came to be and focusing on the only bright spot. The fact that she and Lennox were thrilled about her pregnancy made the rest of it seem, well, unimportant.

She nodded, and he took her hand in his before turning to her parents again. "...and the child she's carrying."

Amara giggled when she saw the stunned looks on her parents' faces. For the first time in her life, she witnessed her mother and father struck speechless. Too delighted to hold back any longer, she chuckled as she watched confusion pass between them. "Mamí, Papí, you're going to be grandparents. I'm pregnant."

"You're grown, Amara," her mother began as she stood next to her, going through the selection of jeweled headpieces the stylist had left. She'd never thought about all these little details for a wedding because she'd never thought about marrying. "You have to make this decision on your own."

"Mamí, they're all so beautiful. How am I supposed to choose?"

Her mother sighed before giving her a look. "I wasn't talking about the headpieces, and I think you know that. Are you sure you're not rushing into this because of the baby?"

She should've known surprise and happiness wouldn't keep her mother quiet for long.

"Neither of us feels compelled to get married because of the baby. Not for the reasons you're thinking anyway. This marriage is strictly about Lennox and me. The baby is a happy gift. We didn't plan on becoming parents, but we're both thrilled this little one is coming."

Her mother nodded, her eyes filling with tears. "If this is what you want, then that's all I care about." Clasping her hands around Amara's, her mother beamed with happiness. "My baby's gonna have a baby. And I'm gonna get to pick out my granny name."

Amara chuckled. "What's wrong with grandma or abuela?"

Her mother jutted her chin in Amara's direction, giving her the same sassy smile Amara often wore. "I'm too sexy and fabulous to be a grandma or an abuela. I need something befitting like noni, or big mama. Maybe even something sophisticated like ma'dea."

"Well," Amara said as she wiped the wet streak from her mother's glowing face. "One thing is obvious to me. Whatever this baby calls you, you're going to end up spoiling it rotten. Aren't you?"

"I spoiled you, didn't I?"

It was true, Amara had never known anything but her mother's love and support, and adoration.

"You sure did."

"Well, considering how wonderful you turned out, I think me spoiling this baby will be just as effective."

Amara took in the sight of her mother glowing as she talked about the baby. And in that moment, she realized Lennox had done her a huge favor in bringing her parents here.

"I'm really glad you and Papí are here, Mamí."

"So am I, baby. So am I." Her mother cleared her throat. "Now, enough of all this sentimental crying. We've got to pick out the perfect headpiece for my perfect baby girl."

Amara knew she wasn't perfect by any stretch of the imagination. But knowing her mother still saw her that way, even after discovering news of her secret wedding, that really was more than she could ever ask for.

Amara stood in front of the mirror taking in her reflection. Of all the outfits she'd ever dreamed about wearing, never had she imagined herself quite like this.

She'd chosen a fitted crepe trumpet gown covered in Swarovski crystals with a plunging neckline and a keyhole back. Every curve on her size sixteen body was on full display and she'd never felt sexier in her life.

She turned to the side to see the small train move and get a glimpse of how the overall design of the dress complemented her shape. She picked up the card that Lennox had sent with the dress and read it again.

*I know you probably would have preferred to choose your own dress. Even though our unexpected nuptials didn't leave you enough time for that, I wanted you to have something you'd like. A quick search, and countless pictures of you in LaQuan Smith's clothing, and I decided to take a chance and see if he could help us out. When he heard it was for you, he said he had the perfect piece. I can't wait to see you in whatever he came up with. I hope it makes up for all the things you'll miss because we didn't have a year to plan a proper wedding.*

*See you on the beach,*
*L.*

The way she looked in this dress more than made up for any loss due to their speedy wedding. Lennox was right, LaQuan Smith was her favorite designer, and this dress fit like he'd made it specifically for her.

Her hair cascaded down over her shoulders. A diamond comb her mother wore on her wedding day tucked some of her dark brown tresses behind one ear.

"Look at my baby!"

Amara turned around to find her mother staring at her with tears threatening to spill from her loving eyes.

"You are a vision. Lennox will be speechless."

She gave her mother a warm a smile and looked behind her. "Where's Papí?"

"He's waiting downstairs to walk you down the aisle. I think he was afraid he'd start crying if he watched you get dressed. He's happy that you're happy. But it's still hard for him to give away his baby girl."

What could she say to that? *Don't worry, Papí, this is only a temporary marriage, and your baby girl will be yours again in four to eight years?* She remained silent, taking a deliberate steadying breath.

"Well, I guess it's time for me to get this veil on and

get downstairs." No matter her reservations, a deal was a deal, and she couldn't back out now. "Time to become Mrs. Lennox Carlisle."

# Thirteen

"My baby's getting married!"

Lennox's mother hadn't been able to contain her excitement since she'd arrived in his hotel room. She ambled over to where he stood in front of a mirror, trying to remember how to tie his necktie.

When she reached him, she placed her hands lovingly on either side of his face, rubbing her thumbs against his cheeks. The tears he saw glistening in her hazel eyes made his chest swell with emotion he wasn't quite sure how to define.

"Mama, don't start crying. You'll ruin all that pretty makeup you have on."

"It's either cry from happiness or wring your neck for lying to me about not seeing someone. You kept a whole girlfriend from me, Lennox. I owe you a behind-whoopin' for that."

He leaned down and placed a quick kiss on her smiling face. "But you won't, because I'm also responsible for you finally becoming a grandmother."

"My baby's having a baby and marrying into a celebrity family. How can I be mad? I'm so happy for you, Lennox. Your daddy, if he were here, he'd be so proud of his boy. Falling in love, starting a family, settling down with the woman he loves, building a strong foundation for the next generation…it's all he ever wanted for you."

"Mama, Amara and I aren't some fairy tale." This wasn't a marriage in the traditional sense. But looking down into his mother's happy face, he realized she had no knowledge of that. To her, her baby boy really was having a whirlwind love affair. He didn't know if this strange feeling was because he was lying to his mother or because in some small way, he was actually happy this was happening. As for his mother, he understood how significant this was for her and decided to just feel happy that he could give it to her. It didn't matter if it was under false pretenses. This was her moment, and he would let her have it.

"Mama, I know Amara and I originally planned to do this alone. But I'm glad you're here."

"I'm glad I'm here, too." She took hold of the loose tie ends and made a beautiful knot. "Otherwise, who would make sure you're camera ready while you wait at the altar?"

Who indeed? There was no one like his mama.

*It's gonna break her heart when this finally comes to an end, and it will be all your fault.*

It was true. It would be his fault. But he still couldn't

bring himself to tell the truth and take away the light shining in her eyes. Not when he'd ached to see it return.

Lennox stood in front of the wedding arch, which was completely adorned with a mix of tropical flowers and white roses, and stared out at the rippling blue waves of the Caribbean Sea. He shoved his hands in the pockets of his cream linen pants, wondering how he'd ended up here.

Of course, he knew the events that had led to him standing at the altar, waiting to make a legal and binding commitment to a woman he barely knew. But what he didn't know was how he'd come to the point where this wedding was anything more than a formality.

He'd like to say it was just because he was playing a role to benefit his mother and Angel's parents. But as he stood here, waiting for the ceremony to begin, he realized the flutters in his stomach weren't caused by dread. No, this was something akin to anticipation, excitement even.

He'd meant it when he'd told Angel this marriage would be real, and they would be together. He would honor the vows he spoke today until their marriage came to the agreed-upon end. He intended to treat Angel with the same respect and care his father had always shown his mother. She was gifting him with a child. In his mind, she deserved no less. But he was beginning to think he actually *wanted* to marry Angel.

*Why, though? It can't just be about the baby.*

He didn't have time to explore that thought, and honestly, he wasn't certain he wanted to. The sound of approaching footsteps pulled him from his musings and forced him back into playing his role as expectant groom. Except, strangely, it didn't feel so much like playing a role at this moment.

"Lennox," Angel Rodriguez called to him just before reaching the arch. "May I have a moment?"

"Of course, Mr. Rodriguez."

"Do we really need to be this formal? You're about to become my son-in-law and the father of my first grandchild."

"Well, since I refer to your daughter as Angel, I feel like family gatherings might get a little confusing if I call you by your given name."

Angel Rodriguez's mouth spread into a wide grin, the same one his daughter wore when she was amused by something. There was warmth there. Considering the situation, Lennox appreciated it.

"Lennox, I won't beat around the bush. I know the reason you and my daughter are marrying so hastily is to protect your career."

Lennox was poised to speak when the older man held up his hand to stop him. "I'm not here to argue the point, Lennox. My daughter has never mentioned anything about wanting to settle down. Her only goal has been to run the legal department for Devereaux Inc. But if she's doing this, she must care a great deal about you. Knowing she doesn't give her heart easily, if she's willing to give hers to you, that speaks volumes to your character."

Lennox stood, staring at the man in awe. He was obviously a proud and protective father, and Angel was lucky to have him. And that made Lennox realize how much he missed sharing a moment like this with his own father.

"Thank you, sir. That means more than you could know."

His future father-in-law nodded and stepped closer to him, slowly raising his hands to Lennox's tie.

*"Ven."* He waved his hand, beckoning Lennox. "Let's straighten your tie. It wouldn't do for you to greet your new bride looking less than perfect."

Lennox complied, stepping closer and letting the older man fiddle with the silk around his neck.

"You might wonder why my wife and I aren't losing our minds about this quickie marriage. Well, in the Devereaux clan, quickie marriages are sort of the norm. You and Amara are no different in that regard. My wife and I married less than six months after we met. It would be hypocritical of us to oppose your union."

Lennox continued to watch the older man's painstakingly slow movements as he fixed Lennox's tie.

"We don't know each other, Lennox. But I hope to change that. I want to be the same kind of father-in-law to you that David Devereaux has been to me. I too had lost my father by the time I married Ja'Net. *Mi papí* held such a special place in my heart, I never thought I'd be able to love another man in that same way. But David filled a void and gave me a way to be a son again, to lay my burdens at my father's feet again."

He finished with the tie, smoothing it, making certain it was tucked neatly inside of Lennox's light gold vest before smoothing his hands on his shoulders and giving them a firm squeeze.

"My baby is my heart, Lennox. And as long as you love, honor and protect her, you'll be mine as well.

Which means I'm here for you too if..." He bowed his head slightly. "If you want me to be, that is."

Lennox's throat was tight. He hadn't felt this much emotion since he'd watched his father's casket lowered into the grave. He'd never thought he could think of another man as a father after losing his own. But at this moment, he certainly didn't mind the offer of a surrogate.

"Sir—"

"Papí." The man reprimanded Lennox with a pointed finger and a fake glare. "Papí, Pops, Dad, or some derivative thereof. Whatever the reason you and my daughter are marrying, it doesn't matter. If she's marrying you, you are family. End of story."

Lennox gave him a wavering smile and reprimanded himself. He was such a jerk. Not just because he'd pushed the man's daughter into an impossible corner, forcing her to marry him. But because as he stood there with this proud man welcoming him into the fold, all Lennox wanted to do was accept everything he was offering him.

The worst part was when Angel's father stepped back and held his arms open, waiting for Lennox to make a decision. Without hesitation, he selfishly accepted everything being offered, even if he was taking it under false pretenses.

"Thank you, Papí."

They embraced until the officiant joined them in front of the arch, telling them the bride was ready.

His soon-to-be father-in-law ended their embrace with an encouraging pat to the arm before he disappeared to join his daughter.

And if the father had just thrown him for a loop, catching the first glimpse of the man's daughter as she stood at the top of the balcony stairs damn near knocked him over.

When he'd contacted LaQuan Smith about sending a dress, he'd had no idea the designer would send what Lennox could only describe as a work of art.

Angel stood alone at the top of the stairs, the picture of elegance, sophistication and outright sex appeal. The formfitting dress with its deep, plunging neckline kept his rapt attention. Even if he'd wanted to look away, he couldn't.

As she descended the stairs and met her father, and the two of them walked slowly toward Lennox on the white sand, he was struck by an unexpected zing of pride. This fierce and self-possessed woman would be his wife. And as much as he knew this marriage was a business decision, he couldn't help but realize how fortunate he was to align himself with someone who understood her own power and unapologetically basked in it.

They might not be in love, but with Amara Angel Devereaux-Rodriguez by his side, he knew they'd be unstoppable.

# Fourteen

"Are you sure you can't stay longer?" Amara asked as she hugged her parents tightly. "We've only just eaten the wedding cake."

Her mother pulled back, smiling at her. "Sweetheart, the cutting of the cake is the traditional end of the wedding. Besides, you're officially on your honeymoon. You don't need your parents underfoot. We wouldn't want to scare Lennox off when we just got him."

"Well…" Amara relented. "Can we at least have breakfast in the morning?"

"Sorry, Mija," her father answered as he placed a quick peck on her cheek. Your mother and I need to be stateside as early as possible. We're leaving before dawn and giving Della a ride back with us. You and Lennox had better enjoy this time together. You know all hell is going to break loose as soon as the Devereauxs find out. Speaking of, when do you intend to tell the family?"

"Can we get past Trey and Jeremiah's wedding next week? They're so excited about their ceremony and Lyric has worked her butt off putting it together in so little time. I'd feel bad about stealing their thunder and making it about Lennox and me."

Her mother lifted a brow, throwing a pointed look in her direction. "So, your plan is to hide your husband for a week? Why?"

"Mamí, the primary is only a few weeks away. I don't want to heap that kind of circus on Trey and Jeremiah. When they get back from their honeymoon, Lennox and I will get the entire family together and tell everyone. I promise."

Never one to interfere in her daughter's private life, Ja'Net simply nodded to bring the subject to a close. The room was abuzz with happiness and family, making her forget how problematic this entire situation was.

All three parents remained a few minutes more to say proper goodbyes to the newlyweds. But when Lennox closed the door to the villa with a resolute click, suddenly, the weight of their reality bore down on her. She was Mrs. Lennox Carlisle for the next four to eight years if her husband became Mayor of New York City.

She cringed at the way she thought about their marriage. Referring to it like she was doing a bid in Sing Sing was a little melodramatic, even for her. Except for when he'd threatened to expose her irresponsible behavior to her grandfather, he'd been nothing but generous and supportive. And considering she was the one who'd been dishonest at their initial meeting, she couldn't say she deserved anything other than his scorn.

He took slow steps back into the living area then just stood there with his vest open and his loosened tie hanging around his neck, his hands casually stuffed inside his cream linen pants. Watching him, she could almost pretend this wasn't what it was—a business deal and nothing more.

"Thank you again for getting our parents down here. Your mother is a gem. I'm so glad I had the chance to meet her."

He scanned her face, looking at her through narrowed eyes. "You make it sound like you're never going to see her again. News flash—you just married her only son and are carrying her first grandchild. You couldn't keep Della Carlisle away with a restraining order at this point."

For some reason, his statement didn't stir as much panic as it should have. She had honestly enjoyed the time she'd spent with his mother today.

"She looked really happy. My parents, too."

She dropped her eyes, fiddling with the heavy diamond wedding set encircling her ring finger. He took her hand in his, causing her to stop twisting her rings and look up at him.

"Our parents being happy about us somehow makes you unhappy?"

"I'm relieved, for sure." She looked up at him and found the weight of his gaze to be too much. She walked to the balcony, hoping to put some distance between them. How could she explain her feelings when she didn't exactly understand them herself?

"Angel?"

She felt his heat before his whisper tickled the base of her neck and sent chills down her spine. He'd followed her onto the balcony.

"I'm not unhappy. I'm just worried about what happens when we divorce."

"We signed a prenup and custody agreement before we married. We know exactly what happens when this marriage ends."

He was right, they had. Their lawyers had been furious to have to jump through so many hoops with so little time to get everything ready. They'd even had both of them sit for a video addendum pledging that neither of them was under any duress.

He moved closer, his body pressing slightly against hers. "Are you cold?"

He took her silence as acquiescence and wrapped her in his embrace. God help her, the feel of him, even when he wasn't necessarily doing anything sexual to her, made goose bumps pebble on her exposed skin.

"I was talking about our parents. I don't think either of us fully appreciated how many people we're going to hurt with our lie."

He slid his hands up her arms and across her shoulders, his thumbs lingering at the base of her neck, rubbing the tension there.

"Angel, I don't know about you, but I hadn't intended on sharing the intimate details of our marriage with our parents. There are some things that should be kept strictly between spouses."

Her nipples pebbled beneath the expensive but thin crepe material of her dress with the barest touch from him. If she were smart, she'd find a way to untangle herself from him. But since she wasn't keen on tumbling over the balcony railing, there was nowhere to go but his arms.

"What do you mean?"

Lennox tightened his hold on her and placed a gentle kiss at the curve of her neck that made her shiver.

"If I must be blunt, I wouldn't share what happens in our marriage bed, so why would I feel compelled to tell them about the sensitive nature of our arrangement? You are my wife, Angel. No matter how that came to be or how it will end, you *are* my wife, and this marriage is very real. I thought we had this conversation already."

She turned around, finally finding the strength to look up into the amber fire in his hazel eyes. "Not that you could, but you promised you wouldn't force me to consummate the marriage unless I wanted to."

He wrapped one hand slowly around her waist, pulling her closer against the bulge tenting his pants. "I am a man of my word. Unless you say otherwise, I will say good-night and head to my room. But that hungry look in your eyes makes me doubt you'll give me my marching papers."

"Cocky, aren't you?"

He shrugged, taking her hand in his and kissing it. "If I remember how we burn everything down around us when we make love, I think I have plenty of reason to be. But if you want me to leave, just say the word."

He took one step back, and before he could take another, she held tight to both ends of his tie, pulling him against her.

"It's dark and it's a long walk across the resort. I

wouldn't want you to get lost on your way back to your room. Perhaps for safety's sake, you should spend the night here, with me. After all, as your wife, your well-being should be paramount to me."

His gaze slid down her face, her neck, and continued down the deep vee of her dress, leaving every inch of skin it touched flushed with desire. Then he lifted his hand to her cheek, stroking the skin gently with his thumb.

"Whatever helps you sleep better at night."

She closed her eyes, trying to steady her heart rate while she fought with herself about what would happen next.

She should tell him to leave, start things as she planned to finish them. But his touch was as intoxicating as the most potent drug, calling to her even when common sense told her to run far, far away.

But when she opened her eyes to find fire burning in his, any thought she had of denying him, denying herself, fell away.

He stepped back, and she placed a hand on his chest, enticed by the rapid pounding of the strong heartbeat beneath it.

"Stay."

She didn't speak another word and was grateful Lennox didn't require her to.

He put his hands on both her shoulders, turning her away from him, gently undoing the intricate fastenings that secured her wedding gown. He tenderly held the fabric as he slid it carefully down the length of her body and waited patiently for her to step out of it when it pooled around her ankles.

Eager to have his skin pressed to hers again, she reached for him, but he held up a finger then picked up her dress and carried it across the room, laying it carefully on the couch.

When he returned, he stopped and took in the full picture of her standing in a silk thong and stilettos. Amara had never been self-conscious about her body. Her curves were a natural part of her, and she had no reason to feel ashamed about them. But as Lennox stared at her, she raised her arms to cover her naked breasts.

Lennox's pinched brow was the only indication of his frustration. He gripped her chin, forcing her to meet his gaze.

"Never hide yourself from me. Everything about your body turns me on."

She kept her arms wrapped around herself, covering her chest. "I don't have issues with my body, Lennox."

"Then why…?"

She dropped her gaze as she tried to figure out the answer to his question. Nothing about it made sense.

"You're a lawyer and a politician, so you should know why. Playing your cards close is a means of survival for people like us. I never have a problem controlling the narrative. Showing people only what I want them to see. But the way you're able to see through all of my defenses, it unnerves me."

"Why? You think I'd hurt you?"

She shook her head without hesitation. Everything she knew about Lennox indicated he was a principled man. Even forcing her to marry him had been so he could continue the work he was doing for the people in his district.

"Not intentionally," she answered. "But this uncontrollable thing between us that makes me do reckless things just to have a taste of what you're offering, I'm afraid of what I'll sacrifice next just to have it. I'm afraid of losing control."

He shook his head. "Angel," the deep rumble of his voice vibrated through her as he leaned close enough to kiss her, "I don't think you're afraid to lose control. I think it's what you want."

She opened her mouth to speak, but nothing came out. She'd spent years negotiating and litigating for the Devereaux empire. But nothing in her arsenal prepared her to respond to a statement like that from a man like him.

"You've always had to think ten steps ahead and do three times as much just to get your grandfather to see your worth. Now you're finally in the position you've always wanted and you're trying to manage everything to secure your place. But there's only one problem, Angel. You can't manage me."

While she tried to gather her wits, he removed his vest, shirt and tie. Before she could anticipate what he was doing, he sealed his mouth to hers in a punishing kiss that left her lungs breathless, and her lips bruised.

"I'd wager to say that's what brought you into Carter's office that first night. That's what keeps this thing burning between us." He devoured her mouth again, pulling her into his arms, holding her tight as he walked her back until the bend of her knees touched the armchair and she soon found herself seated. He ripped his mouth away from hers, leaving them both panting.

"So you're one of those men who gets off on dominating women, making them do your bidding?"

With unwavering confidence, he stared down at her.
"Subservience doesn't do a thing for me. Docile, demure
women may attract some men, but not me. I only keep
strong people in my circle because they push me to be
better. That rule applies to the women I'm attracted to
as well."

He kneeled before her, spreading her knees until he
was pressed between them. He took her hands into his,
placing each on an arm of the chair and pressing them
into the plush cushioned leather.

"I don't get off on bossing you around, Angel. When
we're together like this, the only thing I care about is
giving you what you need. And more than anything,
you need to stop thinking, managing, manipulating and
just feel."

He tapped the backs of her hands with his fingers.
"Keep your hands on the armrests. If you move them,
I stop."

Her gaze lasered in on the almost sinister smile he
wore.

"Stop what?"

"This," he responded as he hooked her thighs over
his forearms and pulled her to the edge of her seat before dipping his head, placing a gentle kiss against her
sex. Even through the silk of her thong, she could feel
the heat of his mouth on her, drawing out the first rip-
ple of pleasure.

Her natural response was to splay her hands on his
bald head and pull him forward until his face was buried between her folds. And by the mischievous stare

he was giving her, he knew it, too. He kept staring, silently daring her to lift even one digit from where he'd placed them.

"Can you give up control long enough to let me please you? Or do we have to fight and fuck like usual?"

Anger-charged sex certainly had its benefits. But there was something about the hungry look in his eyes that promised if she let him have his way, she'd know pleasure like she'd never experienced before.

He took her silence for the acquiescence it was, removing her thong, rubbing his hand slowly up and down her sex as he tugged his bottom lip between his teeth.

Anticipation prickled along every inch of her flesh, making her body tremble even though he'd barely touched her. By the time his tongue slipped between her folds, and he buried two fingers inside of her, she was halfway to climaxing already.

She nearly reneged on her agreement to cede control in this moment. But when the tip of his tongue laved her clit and electric heat spread from her core to the whole of her being like lightning-charged water, she was lost. Each dip of his fingers, scissoring inside of her, caressing her walls with expertly targeted strokes, brought her closer and closer to release.

She felt the uncontrollable shudders, the twitch of her legs. She felt her body tighten around his fingers, the zing of satisfaction building every time the firm, hot flesh of his tongue slid over her sex. She felt it all while crying out against the torture—while begging him to never stop.

She needn't have worried about him stopping, though. He was relentless. That was the only way she could describe the way he pleasured her, never letting up, never slowing down, never missing an opportunity to completely destroy her.

Tension coiled inside of her, her muscles tightening as she dangled over the precipice of completion. And with one final swipe of his tongue, with one final stroke of his fingers stretching her perfectly, she tipped over into bliss, still clutching the arms of the chair, screaming, letting go in a way she'd never before allowed herself.

When the powerful spasms of her climax began to lessen, and conscious thought returned, she wasn't sure if it was a good thing or not to be married to the person that knew how to break her like this. Not when he knew how to own her so completely with so little effort, and especially when she couldn't seem to find the willpower to walk away.

Amara stretched and purred like a cat, cracking her eyes open just in time to see the first rays of the sunrise. Her movement stirred the hard wall of flesh lying behind her, and a thick, corded arm draped itself around her waist, pulling her into a heated cocoon.

"Morning."

Lennox's voice, full of sleep, was rich and deep, and the caress of his breath against her ear made the idea of leaving this bed and his embrace painful.

"What do you want to do today?" he asked.

She laughed at that. They'd been at one of the most exclusive resorts for the last four days. The farthest they'd made it out of her villa was to the private beach for their wedding, and one impromptu evening walk that led to sand getting in places it wasn't supposed to be.

"You mean besides having sex?"

He tightened his arm around her and placed a gentle kiss against her ear.

"You say that like it's a bad thing."

She turned in his arms and instantly regretted it. Until now, their playful banter had felt fun and flirty. But when she met his hazel eyes, everything about the moment they were sharing felt heavy.

"Do you want to go out and see the sights?" He grabbed his phone from the nightstand. "I can make arrangements if you want."

There was something strange in his voice that concerned her, making her raise her hand carefully to his cheek.

"Is there a reason you'd rather stay inside?" She gave his jaw a stroke as she smiled at him. "Besides the obvious, I mean."

"I'm not ashamed of my wife, if that's what you're insinuating. The primary happens soon. If I win, that means constant campaigning for the next five months. I'm sure your desk isn't exactly clear, either. We might not have a quiet moment to ourselves again until the election."

There was something more, something unspoken in his words but still there in his tone. Whatever it was, it made her lean in and kiss him. It was a sweet kiss, meant more to comfort than ignite the passion that sparked so easily between the two of them.

"If you're okay with spending the day inside, so am I."

He snaked one hand around the back of her neck and

placed the other at the small of her back, pulling her on top of him. They'd both fallen asleep naked, which made straddling him so much more fun. Grateful they'd finally had that conversation about foregoing condoms the morning after the wedding, she could already feel the slick of her arousal as her folds came in contact with his already hard length.

The few days they'd spent in this paradise, tucked away on a private beach in the Caribbean away from the world, existing on nothing but fun, relaxation and plenty of sex, had been bliss. If she refused to think about the truth of her situation, she could almost forget this wasn't a proper relationship.

She closed her eyes, wrapping her body tightly around his as hope unwisely grew. Perhaps this relationship, or whatever they were doing, could become more than an arrangement with an expiration date.

Just as that thought began to take root, Lennox's phone rang.

He groaned into her neck before pulling away, groaning again when he looked at the screen to see who was calling. "It's my campaign manager. I have to answer this."

She simply nodded, slipping from the bed and grabbing her silk robe from the foot bench before heading into the bathroom. She glimpsed herself in the mirror on her way to the shower stall. Her lips were kiss-swollen and her curls were in disarray. Though completely debauched, she'd never looked more relaxed and satisfied in her life. But before she could revel in that satisfaction, Lennox knocked on the bathroom door, pulling her away from her thoughts.

"I have to return. One of my opponents in the primary backed out of a Robin Roberts in-depth interview for *20/20*. If I want the slot, I've got to be ready to film by tomorrow morning."

And like a balloon stuck by a sharp pin, her bubble of satisfaction popped.

She swallowed and put on her best smile, the one that told the world everything was fine, even when she knew it wasn't.

"Well, I guess we'd better get packing, then."

He assessed her carefully, then nodded as he left the bathroom. She went back to the mirror, watching as disappointment clouded her eyes and she realized something that should've been obvious from the start. This marriage was a business transaction. If she didn't hold fast to that particular truth, she'd find herself in more trouble than a marriage of convenience, a threat to her career and an unexpected baby could bring. If she wasn't careful, she'd lose her heart.

# Fifteen

"And I think that does it for the interview prep."

Lennox gave a friendly smile to the young man sitting across the table from him in the studio's green room with a clipboard and a pen in his hand.

Lennox zeroed in on the man's work badge to double-check his name. "Thank you, Brian."

Lennox was usually good with names and giving his attention to people when they were speaking to him. But ever since he'd had his driver drop off his new bride outside of her brownstone, he'd had trouble focusing.

He absentmindedly twisted the large wedding ring on his hand. He tried to pretend it was just because wearing the piece of metal against his skin was new. But the truth was, he'd found himself doing it consistently since he and Amara had parted ways.

"Is that real or just for decoration?"

Brian's question pulled him out of the cloud of thoughts filling his head. "It's real. I took a few days off and my fiancée and I got married in the Caribbean."

Brian nodded, granting Lennox a wide grin. "Congratulations," he said brightly as a glint of something akin to excitement mixed with hunger sparked in his eyes. "Are you willing to discuss your recent nuptials during filming with Ms. Roberts?"

Lennox kept his features cool as he pondered the question. Amara wanted to wait until after her cousin's wedding this week to break the news. But the media being as relentless as they were, he wasn't sure they'd be able to keep this quiet. Perhaps the best way to control the story was to share the information on his own terms.

"Sure," Lennox said easily. "I have nothing to hide. Just one question. When will this air? There are people in our family we haven't told yet and we'd like to share the good news with them first before it's all over the airwaves."

"Tomorrow night." The man scribbled something else on his clipboard and gave Lennox a farewell nod. As soon as Brian left, Lennox pulled out his phone and dialed Amara.

"Hey, is everything okay?"

Her greeting was strange. "Everything's fine. Why would you think there was a problem?"

"Because you just dropped me off. Did you need something?"

There was a cool tone to her voice that he'd noticed since they'd boarded the charter jet back to New York.

With no time to discover its source, he simply cleared his throat and continued.

"Nothing's wrong. My wedding ring was just spotted by Robin Roberts's assistant and now they want to talk about our wedding during the filming. The show will air tomorrow."

"But I wanted to tell my family after Trey and Jeremiah's wedding this weekend."

"I know that, Angel. But we either control the story ourselves or risk some paparazzi breaking the story in a salacious way. It's still early. How about you gather your clan today and we tell them about the wedding and the baby?"

She was quiet, and that unnerved him. "Angel, you still there?"

"Yes, I am. Fine, I'll talk to my family."

"No," he responded. "We'll talk to your family, together."

"I'll make the arrangements."

She ended the call without a goodbye and the coolness of her tone raked against his nerves. Whatever this was about, he didn't have time to deal with it now. Brian had returned and was motioning for Lennox to follow him out of the greenroom. He just hoped this wasn't a sign to come of what married life would be like.

Lennox parked in front of Devereaux Manor, shutting off the ignition before turning his gaze to Amara. Aside from rubbing her right thumb repeatedly over the back of her left hand, she hardly moved.

"Is everything okay?"

She met his gaze calmly. "Sure. Why do you ask?"

He pointed to her hands in her lap. "Either you're practicing strumming a guitar on the back of your hand, or that's a nervous tell."

She immediately pulled her hands apart, the action allowing him to see her bare ring finger.

Something ugly flashed in him. He twisted in his seat to face her, fighting hard to keep the dark and dangerous storm brewing inside him from taking over.

"You wanna tell me what's up with that?"

"What's up with what?"

He reached across the console, taking her left hand in his and rubbing his thumb across her bare marriage finger.

"This," he answered with his teeth held tightly together. "Where are your rings, Angel?"

"I haven't lost them, if that's what this is about."

"It's about the fact that we're married and you're walking around with nothing on your finger as if we're not."

She pulled her hand away from his and waved it dismissively in the air. "Expensive jewelry doesn't make us married, Lennox. The little piece of paper we brought back from Jamaica does."

When he failed to respond, she blew out an annoyed breath and dug around in her purse for a few seconds. Then she pulled her hand out, opening her fingers to reveal both her rings cushioned against her palm.

"See, you don't have to worry. They're here."

Silently, he plucked the rings from her hand, turned them over and effortlessly slid the rings over her knuckle and into place.

"For however long we are husband and wife, you will wear my rings and I will wear yours."

"You can't possibly be upset about this. We both know this isn't a real marriage, Lennox. I don't see the need in keeping up pretenses every moment of the day."

The muscle in his eye jumped as if someone had punched him. He could tell from the relaxed look on her face that the punch she'd landed wasn't intentionally thrown. Hell, even he questioned why this was upsetting him so much. But logic be damned, it did bother him.

"This marriage may have an expiration date, but for as long as it exists, it's real. I expect you to wear these so that people across the street can see that you're otherwise spoken for. I will not be made a fool of in public, Angel. You'd do well to remember that."

Shocking himself with such an unusual display of possessiveness, he dropped her hand and settled back into his seat, staring out at nothing and taking a deep breath. When he felt he had control of himself again, he turned back to her, nodding.

"Shall we?"

A spark of fire flashed in her deep brown eyes, turning them a chestnut brown. He'd seen the same fire every time desire blazed between them. But as she twisted the rings on her finger and gave him a cool nod, her mask comfortably settled back over her face. He realized this wasn't passion, it was controlled anger, a warning he might want to proceed with caution.

Amara was a formidable opponent in business and a formidable partner in bed. But no matter how powerful she was, he would not, in any way, allow her to dismiss their marriage in front of anyone.

For the briefest moment he considered he'd possibly come on too strong. But he couldn't relent. He was a proponent of teaching people your boundaries so there was no confusion later. She'd gotten them into this with her lies of omission, so she would meet the expectations he'd laid out to her before they married. Because he would allow no one, absolutely no one, to make him look like a fool. Not even his beautiful wife who tempted him beyond good reason.

"Cousin!"

Stephan was the first one she saw when she walked into Devereaux Manor with Lennox two steps behind her. He surrounded her with a tight hug and kissed her cheek. She lingered in the hug longer than she should have for two reasons. First, soon enough, Stephan would return to Paris, and she'd miss his wonderful hugs. The second and most significant reason was that she needed his support. She knew no matter what she said today, her cousin would back her.

She stepped out of his embrace and made eye contact with the other cousins in the room. Lyric stood near the fireplace smiling at Amara with a wide, comforting grin. Jeremiah and Trey were on the opposite side of the room sharing their warmth and support for her with twin smiles and raised glasses in their hands.

Watching those four people, she knew that whatever resistance she met today, the four of them would have her back. And then she looked to her right and saw the greatest boon of all: her uncle Ace sitting in an armchair with wide-open arms, waiting for her.

She went to him, fortifying herself with his love,

taking an extra squeeze before she let her eyes meet her grandfather's questioning gaze. David Devereaux knew something was up, but as her mother placed a gentle hand on her grandfather's shoulder, silently telling him to back off, Amara understood she could and would do this.

"Everyone, thank you so much for dropping everything and gathering here. It's been an odd but significant last few days, and I wanted to share some new developments in my life with the people I love."

She didn't have to look behind her to know that Lennox was standing close. She could feel his distinct heat enveloping her. It was heady and empowering, helping her forge ahead with their plan.

"I know this will seem strange to most of you, considering how focused I've been on work. But, as my parents and the elders of our family have always told me, work isn't enough. Family, I'd like to introduce you to Lennox Carlisle, my husband and the father of my unborn child."

The room was silent. Considering the Devereauxs always had something to say, concern began to make the skin on her arms prickle. She didn't know how he'd sensed it, but Lennox chose that moment to place a gentle hand around her waist, drawing her in and placing a sweet kiss on her temple.

She looked up into his hazel eyes as everyone in the room stared at them. He was silently telling her, *Don't focus on them, focus on me.* It was the best advice, because as long as she stared into his comforting gaze, she didn't have to deal with her grandfather's glare.

"Oh, my goodness!" Lyric squealed, running over

to the two of them and grabbing them into an excited hug. "Congratulations, Cousin! I'm so happy for you. But first things first, let me see the rings."

Lyric's celebratory mood broke the uncomfortable silence as the rest of her cousins watched her carefully, but slowly began to surround them and offer congratulations. Everyone except her uncle Ace, who blew her a kiss and gave her a knowing wink, as if he'd finally gotten the treat he'd been longing for. And then there was her grandfather, sitting next to Ace, watching her through hooded eyes with not a single glimmer of happiness, glee or even surprise. Apparently, this wasn't over by a long shot.

Stephan stepped in front of them, giving Lennox a strong handshake before leaning over to Amara, wrapping her in one of his tight hugs.

"I don't know what's going on," he whispered in her ear as he nearly swallowed her in his embrace. "But whatever it is, I've got your back. When you're ready to tell me, you know I'm here."

She latched on to Stephan like the anchor he was, the anchor he'd always been, holding her up when the ground beneath her seemed to fall away. She gave him one more squeeze then stepped back, feeling the slightest bit better.

"Damn, girl, I thought Jeremiah and I were moving fast. You've got us beat," Trey teased from her spot near the fireplace. Amara hadn't known her new cousin long, but in the short time she'd been around, she and Amara had become family in more than name only. "I don't know about anyone else, but I need details. When, where and how did all of this take place without any of us nosy folks being the wiser?"

"Lennox and I took one look at each other, and we just knew." That was the most truthful response Amara could come up with. But she'd never imagined in such a short time she'd end up pregnant with his child and married to him.

"We didn't want to wait, but I didn't want to steal your and Jeremiah's thunder with your wedding coming up this week," Amara continued. "So, we eloped to Jamaica and married in a small ceremony on the beach with the ocean and the sunset as our backdrop with our parents by our sides."

Lyric sighed loudly enough that everyone in the room turned to her. Her face was bright with wide eyes that sparkled as her eyelashes fluttered.

"That's so romantic!"

"It absolutely was," Amara's mother responded as she stood up and walked to the doorway. "In celebration, I had a replica of their wedding cake made. Lennox's family should be here shortly. Della texted me a little while ago to say she and her daughter and daughter-in-law will arrive soon. We'll cut the cake when they get here."

"How did you have time to do all of this, Mamí?"

Her mom blew a kiss her way before leaving the room, and the tension twisting the muscles at the base of Amara's neck loosened just a bit. Lennox chose that moment to slide his hand down her back, leaning in to place a kiss on her temple.

"Why don't you have a seat? A lot has happened in the last few days. I don't want you tiring yourself out."

She looked into his eyes and saw what looked like genuine concern. And for the brief moment that their gazes connected, she wanted to believe all that worry and consideration was for her. But the small voice pulling at the back of her brain wouldn't let her reach for that hope. Not when she knew there was an expiration date on their union. This marriage was about the baby and his career. There was no room for her or what she wanted. Not that she had any clue what that was.

"I'm gonna go check in on my mom for a sec. You wanna join me, or are you okay with being in the middle of the lion's den?"

He chuckled softly and nodded. "Believe me, I've dealt with worse. I'm a politician, remember. Schmoozing tough crowds is kinda my thing. Go check on your mom. I'll be fine."

Amara left the room, feeling every eye following her as she went through the archway into the hall. By the time she found her mother in the kitchen, her fingers and limbs tingled with relief.

"Mamí, you didn't have to go through this trouble to get us a cake."

"Hush," her mother chided, never once taking her eyes off the cake as she removed the protective box. "My baby just got married. If I can't play the mother of the bride at a big wedding, then I'm surely going to do it here amongst family."

Amara flinched at her mother's comment. "Are you upset we didn't have a big wedding?"

Her mother stopped her fiddling and looked directly at Amara. "Baby, how and when you married was completely up to you. I'm just glad I could be part of it. As long as you're sure this marriage is what you want, I'm thrilled to play any role I can in celebrating it. You are still sure this marriage is what you want, aren't you?"

Amara was about to reassure her mother when the familiar baritone of her grandfather's voice vibrated through the room.

"That's certainly a fair question, considering this marriage happened out of thin air."

"Daddy, leave that child alone."

Amara raised her hand to stop her mother from leaping into mama bear mode. "It's okay, Mamí. It's understandable that Granddaddy has questions."

"I have quite a few questions, Granddaughter. Namely, how the hell did you end up married to the city councilman we need to make this Falcon deal happen?"

"I went out for a drink and ran into Lennox. We hit it off. Once we spent time together, we realized our connection went deeper than business."

Her grandfather's face was pulled into tight lines. She could see suspicion clouding his eyes.

"And the deal? In your zeal to be together, did either of you think about the conflict of interest you were willingly walking into?"

"Yes, Grandfather." The formal name slipped from her lips, and she could see him brace against it. Too bad if he didn't like it. She didn't like being interrogated about her personal life, so they were even as far as she was concerned. "We thought about it and came up with a reasonable solution. We will use a third-party review panel to decide if we get the permits or not. It's the only way we can ensure that things happen in a fair manner."

Her grandfather narrowed his eyes into tiny slits as

he tried to see the holes in her lies. Her story was solid, and she knew it. But that didn't mean David Devereaux was buying any of it.

He stepped closer to her, placing his hand carefully on her forearm as he looked down at her.

"Marriage is sacred, Amara. It's not something you should take lightly. Whatever it is you've gotten yourself into, I hope it doesn't come back to haunt you. You've got so much more on the line now than a business deal. The decisions you've made affect that little one you're carrying, too. Make sure you know what you're doing."

Everything in her wanted to flinch at his warning, but she refused to give him the satisfaction. She already questioned her decisions and how they would impact her baby. She didn't need him reminding her of how she'd screwed up yet again.

"Did you question how fast Trey and Jeremiah decided to marry? The only difference is they apprised the Devereauxs of their relationship. We know what we're doing. This is our decision, and it doesn't require anyone else's approval."

There was a cold glint in her grandfather's eye. "If that's your final word on the matter, then I guess I'll have to accept it. But hear me, Amara. If for one moment I think Devereaux Inc. is in danger because of the decisions you've made, I won't hesitate to remove you and reinstate myself as lead counsel. Do you understand me?"

Fire burned beneath her skin but she had to remain in control at all costs. This was a power play, and she couldn't afford to lose.

"I've earned this position. You didn't give it to me. If

you didn't question Jeremiah's ability to lead as co-CEO upon discovering his involvement with Trey, don't question mine regarding my husband. Devereaux Inc. will thrive under my leadership in the legal department. Just stand back and watch."

She stiffened her spine ramrod straight and stepped out around her grandfather into the hall. She would prove him wrong, no matter what it took. Because the best motivation in the world was for someone to tell her she shouldn't or couldn't do something. She would make David Devereaux eat his words. Even if the personal cost was more than she could bear.

# Sixteen

Lennox looked from one side of his living room to the other. Every surface was covered with laptops and papers, every seat was taken, and the volume of the television above his fireplace was so loud, it was as if Anderson Cooper was personally yelling at him from the CNN newsroom.

He rubbed the tight muscles of his neck, trying to stave off the tension headache he could feel coming on. He had no one to blame but himself. He knew that lack of sleep, too much caffeine and too little food always resulted in a pounding headache that made him miserable to be around.

"Hey." Carter tapped him on the shoulder before handing him a cup of coffee and sitting down next to him. "You okay?"

Lennox sipped his coffee, hoping that if he focused on his drink long enough his friend would forget his question.

"I know you heard me."

No such luck, apparently. Lennox pushed aside some of the papers cluttering the end table next to his chair and gently rested the coffee mug on it.

"I'm fine, Carter." He gave his friend a practiced smile before he began twisting the wedding band on his finger. He'd never been one for jewelry. Other than his class ring from law school, he rarely wore any. But somehow the thick, smooth platinum band felt so natural to him, he found himself touching it, making sure it was still where it was supposed to be ever since Angel had put it there.

"Nah." Carter shook his head. "I've seen fine and this ain't it. What's up?"

"If you haven't noticed, I'm kind of busy waiting for primary results to find out if I'll actually make it as a candidate for mayor."

Carter sipped his coffee, then nodded slowly. "I had. But we both know you've got nothing to worry about with the primary. This race has been yours since you entered it. The only thing that could've derailed it—" he jutted his chin out in the direction of Lennox's wedding ring "—you handled. So, if I could hazard a guess, I'd say it's more personal than professional."

Carter made a show of looking around before he met Lennox's gaze again. "Where's Amara? I was hoping to get to meet my best friend's new surprise wife. Everything okay on the home front?"

Lennox looked around to make sure all of his campaign staff were otherwise occupied. Most of them knew he'd recently married, but none of them knew the circumstances and Lennox wanted to keep it that way.

He picked up his mug, stood and beckoned his friend to follow him to his study.

He waited until Carter closed the heavy door and they were secure inside the dim space with its mahogany walls. He sat on the edge of his desk as Carter sat on the leather couch against the wall.

"Things not so perfect in paradise?" Carter began, picking up right where he'd left off in the living room.

"Angel and I are fine."

"Well, you're still using her nickname, that's a good sign. But if you're fine, where is she? She's your wife. Don't you think it's strange that she's not standing by your side as you wait for the results?"

Lennox took another sip of his coffee as he thought about the answer to that question. Yes, he and Angel were husband and wife. But their relationship wasn't exactly traditional. Other than his expectations of fidelity, and the duration of their marriage, he hadn't added any terms that concerned situations like these.

"Angel has a job, too. She's head of corporate legal at Devereaux Inc. I can't expect her to just drop everything and come babysit me while I freak out about the results."

Carter lifted a brow as he tilted his head, giving his full attention to Lennox. "Of course, you can. She's your wife. If you need her here, she should be here."

"If she wanted to be here, she would be. I'm not about to force her to do anything she doesn't want to do."

*You didn't have a problem forcing her to marry you when it suited. Why the hesitation now?*

He ground his teeth as his conscience reminded him of his actions.

"Knowing you, Lennox, you didn't even ask her to take the day off to be with you."

His friend had him there. No matter how much he'd wanted her to stay before she walked out the door this morning, he couldn't give in to that desire. It would mean he needed her, the way his mother needed his father. And his mother had lost everything when his father died; Lennox couldn't afford to be dependent on Amara like that.

"Carter, I appreciate you trying to help, man. But I know what I'm doing. Angel and I are fine. I'm fine."

"You keep saying that, but somehow I'm not convinced." Carter stood up, heading for the door. "Call your wife, man. If for no other reason than it will look strange to any reporters that may happen by."

Lennox took one final look at his friend, nodding his head as he grabbed his phone. Carter turned to him once more, pointing an accusatory finger at him.

"Oh, and Nevaeh said she wants to meet her new *tia.* If you know like I know, you'd better make that happen. Nothing will ruin your world like a five-year-old who's mad with you."

Lennox chuckled as Carter left. Nevaeh was definitely a handful on her best day, and she'd rip him to shreds if he crossed her. But that little one was his heart. As her godfather, it was his job to keep a smile on her face.

Feeling a little less unsettled, Lennox sent up a silent prayer of thanks that his friend had given him an excuse for calling his wife. At least now he could pretend it was all about preserving their ruse for the media and not about the fact that he needed her by his side. Because never, not as long as he drew breath, would he allow himself to admit he needed her for anything more than his professional image and physical satisfaction.

Amara watched as Lennox's name flashed across her cell phone's screen. A heady mix of anticipation and apprehension swirled inside her. Today was the primary. Today, they'd know if the people would choose him to represent their party in the upcoming mayoral race.

She tapped the screen connecting the call, clearing her throat to stabilize the tremors in her voice.

"Hey, how's it going?"

"That's a strange way for a wife to greet her husband, don't you think? Shouldn't you know how I'm doing? Oh wait," he interrupted himself. "That would mean you actually seeing me, which you haven't done since we announced our marriage to your family."

"Lennox, I can't just drop everything. I work, too. Or did you forget why I agreed to this marriage in the first place? Also, my cousins are getting married this weekend. I'm busy."

"I wasn't suggesting that you aren't." He blew out a long breath. His voice sounded slightly less irritated when he spoke again. "I'm sorry, Angel. I was being an ass. I'm just…"

"You're on edge about the primary, right? I'm sure you've got a roomful of people around you to help you relax. Make them earn their keep."

He was quiet, too quiet. She held her breath, waiting for his response.

"You're right, there is a roomful of people. But none of them is my wife."

There was something in the way he said the word *wife* that cut through her. There was a longing there that made a gentle ache spread through her.

"Well, I know we agreed I'd be officially moved into your place by the wedding, but I guess I could stop packing long enough to come over while you watch the returns."

Again, more silence, then another breath. "Thanks" was all he said before he disconnected the line. But that simple word felt heavy, filled with so much unexplained emotion that even after the call ended, she was still standing there trying to process what exactly was happening.

*Guess you'll find out when you get there.*

Amara found Lennox on his balcony with the sleeves of his white button-down shirt rolled up to the middle of his forearms and his hands shoved in the pockets of his slacks.

She could see the tension vibrating off him in waves. Lennox always came off confident and self-assured. Save for the time he tried to convince her to take a pregnancy test because of his mother's premonition, this was the first time she'd ever seen him look less than in control.

She stepped closer to him, placing a light hand against his bare forearm when she stood next to him. "The last I checked, you were ahead. Has that changed?"

His stiff shoulders dropped as he released a soothing breath. "No, I'm still ahead."

"Then what's wrong? You sounded tightly wound on the phone, but this is way worse than a little angst."

"Did I ever tell you how I got into politics?"

She shook her head.

"I was a corporate attorney for many years. It paid me very well, as you know from firsthand experience. But it left me empty.

"My father was a local politician with a focus on the city councilman's office. That might sound short-sighted, but his heart was only ever in helping the people locally in his beloved city. We were pushed out of our home by a big conglomerate who didn't care that we were a poor family barely hanging on. They just came in, threw their money around and brought in more people with lots of money to take our place. It took us years to get back on our feet. But it sparked a fire in my father to fight for a voice in what happened to his neighborhood. So, he ran for smaller offices until he finally became the representative for his neighborhood."

Amara hadn't known any of that. It explained why Lennox was so hell-bent on keeping companies like Devereaux Inc. on a tight leash.

"And now you've protected his neighborhood and are moving on to taking care of his city. You should be proud, Lennox."

He turned to her, scanning her face as if he were searching for something. Then he leaned down, pressing his mouth against hers. The kiss was more comforting that sensual, yet it still made her heart pound hard underneath her rib cage.

"What was that for?"

He pulled his thumb across her bottom lip before looking out across the cityscape.

"For being here. I've been in my head a lot today. Thinking about what happens next if I win the primary race." He huffed, closing his eyes for a brief second before returning his gaze to hers. "My father's political career started because he wanted to create a better situation for my sister and me. When I entered this race, I would've said I was doing it to continue my father's legacy."

"That's changed?"

He shrugged, leaning against the railing. "I'm about to become a father. Everything has changed. I want to make a difference in this city for all my constituents. But mostly, I want to make a better one for the child you're carrying. I have this sudden need to make everything better before the baby gets here. And all day I've been wondering what will happen to my child if I fail. Knowing this baby is coming raises the stakes of this primary and the election in the fall. There's so much more on the line."

So this was what his moodiness over the phone was about. She found herself stepping into his embrace, wrapping her arms around him as she laid her head against his chest.

As surely as she knew her own name, she knew that she and this baby were lucky Lennox was its father. He was annoyingly condescending, controlling, and downright rude at times when he dealt with her. But he was also tender with her in ways that made her feel precious.

Her head warned her about falling for this man. All

of his concern was for the child she carried and not for her directly. But even knowing that wasn't enough to stop her from diving headfirst into the rippling ocean that was Lennox Carlisle. More than anything, she wanted to be swallowed whole by him.

"Lennox," she whispered so softly she didn't think he could hear her. But when he tightened his arms around her, she knew he had. "Whether you win or lose, this baby is going to be lucky you're its dad. Despite all the rough patches we've had, I'm glad I get to coparent with a man who cares this much about the community he lives in."

He peered down into her face with unanswered questions burning in his eyes.

"Angel—"

He didn't have a chance to finish as a loud commotion erupted from inside the apartment.

"Boss!" A man Amara recognized as Lennox's campaign manager made his way through the small crowd until he was standing directly in front of them. "CNN just projected you as the winner of the primary race. You're in the running for Gracie Mansion!"

She looked up at Lennox just in time to catch a grin so wide and bright spreading across his face that her breath caught in her chest, and she felt the slightest bit dizzy.

She tried to pretend it was pregnancy hormones that had her feeling so light-headed. But then that everpresent voice in the back of her mind tapped her on her shoulder like a little devil, or angel, she couldn't tell which just yet.

*You know doggone well this ain't got a thing to do*

*with that baby. Go'n and admit. That man's happy smile just made you swoon.*

*Amara girl*, the voice bellowed in her head. *You'd better watch out.*

She'd certainly better.

# Seventeen

"Amara?"

Lennox perked up when a woman in floral scrubs called his wife's name.

"Are you coming with me?"

Lennox looked up at a now standing Angel as she gazed down at him with a furrowed brow.

"I wasn't sure you'd want me to."

A generous smile lifted the corners of her lips, calming some of the anxiety he'd experienced since arriving at her ob-gyn's office.

"Lennox," she whispered as she extended her hand to him. He stood, grabbing her hand and letting her lead him through the doorway to the examination room.

Once they were there, the nurse led Angel behind a partition while he sat in a chair next to the exam table, taking in all the instruments and machines.

He took a deep breath, attempting to steady himself, trying to decipher what he was actually feeling. From the moment they'd discovered her pregnancy, Lennox's heart had ached with anticipation of this child's entrance into the world. But he hadn't counted on the fact that Angel would want him by her side every step of the way.

He was grateful for the chance to participate, thrilled to learn about the development of their child firsthand, but there was something unsettling about being here that kept intruding on the joy and excitement of this moment.

Angel rejoined him dressed in a cloth hospital gown. As soon as he saw her, his chest tightened. It was at that moment he understood what that thing was that kept picking at what should be one of the happiest moments of his life. It was fear. Fear of this bonding exercise that would make it harder to walk away from her when he had to.

Refusing to think more about it, he swallowed the lump in his throat, standing and extending his hand to her as she lay back on the exam table.

A smiling woman with a short pixie cut and a white lab coat entered the room. She stared at Lennox as if she were attempting to figure out the answer to an equation. "Hello, Amara and…"

"I'm Lennox Carlisle, her husband."

The woman nodded and extended her hand to him. "I'm Dr. Bautista. Forgive me for staring, but you look very familiar."

Angel chuckled, relieving some of the tension in the room.

"He's running for mayor. You've probably seen his face on posters all over Brooklyn."

The doctor nodded again, shaking his hand, then taking her seat on the stool next to the exam table.

"Today I'm going to do a transvaginal sonogram to confirm proper placement and development of the fetus as well as gestational age. According to the information on your intake form, you believe you're approximately eight weeks along?"

"I'm fairly certain." Angel looked up at Lennox and winked, drawing a knowing smile from him.

"All right," the doctor continued. "Let me wash my hands and we'll get started."

Lennox returned to his seat and watched silently as the doctor went through the process. He had no idea what to expect, and as blotchy images began to form on the dark monitor, he stiffened with anticipation.

Angel took a deep breath, drawing him out of his own musings. She was nervous, too. Honestly, she had a right to be. She was doing all the heavy lifting in this scenario. It was his job to reassure her and support her through these moments.

He slid his hand into hers and noted some of the tension left her. Her calm spilled back over onto him in a feedback loop, solidifying their partnership in ways he couldn't explain. They really were in this together. Success or failure, this was all on them as a team.

The doctor pointed at the monitor and smiled.

"Amara and Lennox, it's my pleasure to introduce you to your little one."

Lennox stared at the screen, trying to decipher the mixture of black and gray spots and then, suddenly, a tiny gray tadpole jumped out at him.

"Is that…?"

"Yes, it is." The doctor smiled as she looked up at him. "And if you think that's a neat trick, just wait until you hear this."

Dr. Bautista fiddled with some of the controls on the machine's keyboard and suddenly a sound like a miniature jackhammer filled the room.

Lennox looked down at his wife in awe. Angel's eyes looked like liquid glass as tears spilled from them. His own heart rate picked up and he wondered if he could withstand this level of excitement.

"Lennox, do you hear that? It's our baby's heartbeat."

"It sounds strong." He smiled down at her, too drawn in by their shared happiness to let any misgivings about their relationship mar this precious moment. Not caring that they weren't alone, he leaned down, placing a grateful kiss on her lips.

He realized his face was wet with what he thought were Angel's tears. But as he pulled away from the kiss and fresh hot drops slid down his face, he understood they were his.

As a politician, he'd learned long ago to keep his emotions hidden in public. But in this moment, the cloak of respectability and restraint fell away as he touched his forehead to his wife's and celebrated.

The doctor cleared her throat, interrupting to give them all the details of her findings and what the next steps were. When she was done, she slipped quietly from the room.

As soon as Angel sat up, Lennox sat down next to her on the table, pulling her into his arms, kissing her, hoping each press of his lips articulated all the things he couldn't say like *thank you*, and *I'm happier than I've ever been in my life*, and *I love you*.

That last one made his brain snap to attention, doing its best to swim through the dopamine haze. He pulled himself back, ending the kiss, locking eyes with Angel as if he were seeing her for the first time. And in part, he truly was.

He'd never thought love would be a word he associated with her. But looking at her, the realization filled his heart and pumped out into his blood vessels, seeping into every cell of his being. He was in love with his wife.

*So*, his mind began, *what are you gonna do now, Lennox?*

Panic clawed at him as he pulled Angel into his embrace and held on as tightly as he dared without risking hurting her.

*I have no idea.*

Lennox was quiet. He'd been quiet since they'd left the doctor's office and all through the ride back to his home.

"Is everything all right?" she asked as they walked through the door.

He turned around with raised brows and met her gaze.

"Sure," he replied. "Why wouldn't it be?"

She shrugged, assessing him, trying to see past his defenses.

"You've just been quiet since we left my appointment. Are you having regrets? I know the sonogram probably made this child real to you in ways you hadn't anticipated. It certainly has for me."

He stepped closer to her, placing a gentle hand on her cheek.

"Angel, my feelings about this baby haven't changed. If anything, seeing the sonogram and hearing our baby's heartbeat made me even more determined to be here with you."

Her heart felt like it had grown too big for her chest wall, pushing against the confines of her ribs. She saw hope floating in the depths of his eyes. Hope she reminded herself she couldn't chance reaching for. This wasn't about her, only their child.

"I'm more committed to this baby than ever."

Those were the words any mother should want to hear from their child's father. But somehow they only seemed to highlight the painful truth of their relationship. He wanted their baby, and Amara was a convenient afterthought.

She pulled her gaze from his, afraid he'd see the disappointment she felt clutching to the edges of her good mood.

"Glad to hear it." She looked down at her watch, finding the excuse she needed to end this awkward moment. "I've got to get to work and finish up some things."

"Will you be returning here tonight, or are you still pretending you're packing?"

The smile on his face was contagious and she nearly laughed aloud. "Everything I'm bringing with me is already here. I just need to know what bedroom you want me in."

He nodded, turning down a long hall and beckoning her to follow him. At the very end of it was a set of double doors that he opened up, ushering her inside.

"This is the master. You can have it."

"Have it? Is this where you sleep?"

He pushed his hands into his pockets. "It is, but it's the only room with an en suite bathroom." When she threaded her brows together to silently ask why that mattered, he continued. "According to the literature I've been reading, frequent trips to the bathroom are to be expected. With all the prep for the primary, I haven't had a chance to move my things into the guest room, but I'll try to get it done soon."

"This is very kind of you, Lennox. But are you sure?" She looked around the room, her gaze colliding with the large platform bed sitting in the middle of the room.

She pulled her eyes away from it quickly. The one thing she didn't need was the image of Lennox spread out in this bed with nothing but a sheet covering up all that golden skin of his.

"You don't have to worry, Angel. I promised the only thing I'd demand from you as your husband was that we share a residence and present a united front in public. Anything else that happens, happens because we both want it. I'll never take what you're unwilling to give."

She swallowed as she looked at him. His face was pulled into tight lines, emphasizing how serious he was about the subject. If only he knew she wasn't as unwilling as he believed.

Amara wanted her husband. But since he hadn't approached her for sex since they'd returned home, she'd figured their little honeymoon romp was over.

"And what if I'm willing?"

He let his gaze caress her like an appreciative hand.

Her nipples pebbled beneath her shirt. Hello, pregnancy-enhanced libido.

He must have noticed the turgid peaks beneath the soft cotton of her shirt, because his gaze burned through the material, searing her without the benefit of touch.

"What is it you're trying to tell me, Angel?"

She never had a problem articulating her thoughts. She saw no reason to beat around the bush now.

"I'm saying, I want sex. And I explicitly remember you telling me if I needed it, you'd gladly supply it. Are those still the terms of our agreement?"

He didn't answer, at least not verbally. With two long strides he was in front of her, threading his fingers into her hair and pressing his lips against hers. His other hand snaked up her side and he ran his thumb across her nipple. Her sex clenched, eliciting a deep moan that made her wonder who else was in the room with them, because there was no way such a hungry needy sound came from her.

She briefly recognized how easily all sense of decorum and decency disappeared. Later she might lament how little it took for her to succumb to her baser needs whenever he put his hands on her. But right now, all she could focus on was the fire his kisses were stoking in her.

If she was honest, she'd acknowledge the joy she'd experienced when they'd witnessed their baby for the first time, heard its heartbeat, had changed something between them. Watching what they'd created thriving inside of her, it was like a heavy lock clicking into place, binding her to Lennox on every plane of her existence.

And once he'd kissed her, each press of his lips filled

with so much joy, she lost what little control she had over her heart.

Now, she was swooped up in her husband's arms and carried across the expanse of the large room. He placed her on his bed, stripping her of all her clothes as if he was tearing through wrapping paper to get to the present inside.

His hands roamed frantically over her body, burning her flesh with his touch.

She reached for his length, delighted he was as hard as granite beneath her fingertips. She loved foreplay, but right now, the only thing she wanted was her body wrapped around his.

He didn't make her wait. With no hesitation, he placed himself at her entrance and pushed until he was stretching her wide, touching her in all the hidden spaces only he seemed to know how to reach.

"Damn, baby," he moaned in her ear once he was fully seated inside her. "You never have to ask me for this, Angel."

He began a slow rhythm with his hips, one that teased and tortured her, drawing a keening sound from the depths of her being. It was too much and not enough all at the same time, keeping her in this constant state of need that both excited and frightened her simultaneously.

Out of bed, they couldn't be more different. He was a political do-gooder, and she was a corporate vulture. Their worldviews clashed. But in this bed, while she touched him everywhere her fingers could reach, while he owned every inch of her, they were in perfect sync.

And yet still, she wanted more.

"Please, Lennox."

She couldn't say exactly what she was asking for, couldn't have defined if she'd tried.

He stared down at her, his eyes aflame with a passion mirroring hers. She might have been afraid of it if she didn't feel the same uncontrollable desperation herself.

"You have no idea what it does to me to hear the sound of my name on your lips while I'm buried inside you."

Without warning, he pulled her up and turned her over, the motion throwing off her equilibrium while exciting her at the same time.

Her sex tightened and she lamented the emptiness his absence left. Fortunately, she didn't have to wait long before he was buried inside her again. This time, there was no slow rocking. Instead, he slammed deep inside her from the first stroke.

He laid a strong hand at the base of her neck, pushing her down to deepen the angle until her head rested against the pillow, and when he moved again, his cock slid across that magical knot inside her and the world turned upside down.

With no warning, she climaxed, every muscle she possessed seizing up.

"That's it." He leaned over her, still pounding into her, extending her orgasm, breaking her into tiny pieces from the inside out. "Let go. Let me give you what you need."

He pulled himself upright and she thought he might be kind enough to give her a momentary reprieve to compose herself.

He did not.

Instead, he clasped his fingers so tightly around the

deep curves of her hips she knew there'd be bruising there tomorrow. But she didn't care, because he was sliding back into her, reigniting the flame she'd barely survived the first time around.

And like before, the feel of him, the way he played her body like a master when he reached around, sliding the rough pads of his fingers over her sensitive clit, sent her careening off the jagged edge of a cliff into blinding pleasure that made her body quake uncontrollably.

When her body spasmed around him this time, his pace increased; his thrusts were more forceful, but his rhythm faltered. And as she broke apart for him again, he crashed into his own orgasm, gripping her so tightly, mixing the slightest bit of pain with her pleasure just before he collapsed. His body covered her like a hot weighted blanket that soothed and comforted her while she tried to piece herself back together.

He gathered her in his arms, kissing her mussed hair. Just as she began to drift off into post-coital sleep, she felt his arm draped across her waist as he pulled her closer to him and whispered, "Mine."

Amara shuddered, delighted by the possessiveness of this moment, but afraid this was all just endorphins making him say something he didn't mean. As she snuggled closer to him, placing her hand atop his, with every ounce of her being, she wanted his declaration to be true. Refusing to dig deeper, she closed her eyes and began to drift off to sleep, ignoring her plans to return to work.

Yeah, she'd told herself she was going back. But she figured since this was her first time ditching work for good sex, she was entitled to stay curled up in her husband's embrace.

* * *

Halfway between sleep and consciousness, Amara silently luxuriated in the feeling of heavy warmth pressed against her. She thought about getting up but didn't want to risk disturbing the serenity that lying in Lennox's arms gave her.

She finally opened her eyes when he pressed a light kiss to her bare shoulder. She turned around and when their eyes met, for the briefest moment, the joy she felt building inside was reflected in his gaze. But before she could fully appreciate it, the warmth left his eyes and a cold glare remained.

"I still have some things I need to take care of today."

She lifted up on her elbow to look at the wall clock. "It's almost eight o'clock. Business for the day is over."

"Not when you're a public official." He disentangled himself from her and got out of bed, putting on his underwear and grabbing the rest of his clothing off the floor.

"The fridge is fully stocked if you're hungry."

She was still reeling, trying to figure out how they'd gone from being so cozy to the wide chasm that seemed to be broadening with every article of clothing he picked up.

When he reached the door, he nodded, stopping briefly and looking up at the ceiling before returning his gaze to hers.

"Thank you for allowing me to come with you to the doctor's today. I'd like to attend all your appointments, if you'll allow it."

"Of course," she replied.

"Let me know as soon as you book them, and I'll juggle around my schedule to make sure I'm available."

There was something strange about the way he stared at her, as if he wanted to say more.

She sat up on the bed, pulling the covers over herself, needing a barrier between them.

"Lennox, whatever my hesitation about this marriage, I've never attempted to keep you out of the loop when it comes to my pregnancy. You don't have to ask me to be a father to your child. I appreciate the consideration you're showing me, but there's no need to ever question if I want to share this baby with you."

The stiff set of his shoulders relaxed a little before he nodded and gave her a small smile.

"Thank you for that. This baby really does mean the world to me."

It was the last thing he said before leaving, and once again Amara was left walking a tight line between delight that Lennox wanted to be such an involved father and disappointment that his only focus, even after they'd spent the day making love, seemed to be the child she was carrying and not her.

# Eighteen

"Earth to Lennox."

Lennox looked up into his friend's questioning gaze.

"I'm sorry, Carter. My mind was drifting."

Carter gave him an inscrutable look and then started wiping the bar down. "You know, despite being a guy who was lucky enough to recently marry a gorgeous woman—and, my friend, Amara truly is gorgeous— a man who has a baby on the way, and who just won the primary race for the office he's seeking, this is the second time this week I've caught you looking hang-dog in the face."

Carter was right. Lennox was a lucky bastard who should be at home counting his blessings instead of hiding in his friend's bar avoiding his wife. So why wasn't he?

Because he was a coward. A coward who was becoming more deeply ensnared by the woman he married.

"Angel is gorgeous, and after seeing the baby for the first time, I'm happier than I've ever been."

"Then why are you sitting in my bar instead of at home loving your wife?"

When Lennox didn't answer, Carter regarded him carefully and then nodded his head as if he'd cracked the mystery of Lennox's broken way of thinking.

"That's it, isn't it? It's the loving her part you're having difficulty with?"

Carter and Lennox had known each other too long and been through too much to lie to each other. So there was no use in denying Carter's assertion.

"All I keep thinking about is how destroyed my mother was when my dad died. She may as well have been in the grave with him. What happens when Angel walks away from me? What happens if something happens to her, and I'm left behind? I mean, I know it sounds irrational, but you of all people should understand why my fears are valid."

Carter spread his arms out and braced his hands on the bar. "I do understand what you're thinking. I've lived it. And if I hadn't needed to live to take care of Nevaeh, I don't know if I would've made it when Mish was killed in that accident. But knowing all I do, knowing all the pain I'd eventually suffer after she was gone, I could never regret the love we shared. If I could, I'd choose to love her over and over again."

Lennox wished he was as brave as his friend. But

he wasn't. Being that caught up in someone else scared the hell out of him.

"Before I came here, I was holding Angel in bed after spending most of the day making love to her. And everything felt so right. She turned around and I looked at her, and all I wanted to do was forget about the rest of the world and never leave the safety of that bed."

"Then why did you?"

"Because if I stayed with her that way tonight, I'd do it again the next time and the next time. I'd never be able to let go. So, I got up, dressed and came here."

"Man, listen," Carter scoffed. "For a man with a bunch of fancy degrees, you're not that bright."

Lennox shrugged. "What the hell are you talking about?"

"You've got a boss babe in your bed, and you voluntarily leave her to come sit at my bar and work out your issues? Make it make sense, man." When Lennox waved a dismissive hand, Carter continued. "Let me give you a friendly piece of unsolicited marital advice. Don't mess around and become the subject of an early aughts hip-hop and R & B collaboration track."

"Now I'm really lost. That cleaning fluid you were spraying on the bar top must be getting to your brain."

Carter shook a scolding finger at him. "You know what I'm talking about. The tracks where fellas are trying to be hard and mess around and lose their women and then the R & B crooner has to come on and sing a soft hook to beg for forgiveness."

When Lennox didn't respond, Carter pulled out his phone, scrolled a few times. Suddenly, LL Cool J's 2002 hit "Luv U Better" blared from the elevated speakers mounted in the corners of the main lounge. And to piss Lennox off further, Carter started dancing behind the bar as he sang the lyrics, making a point to look directly in Lennox's face as he did so.

By the time LL, Marc Dorsey and Carter reached the bridge, Lennox felt like trash, which he was certain was the point of his friend's little performance. The only problem was now he was more confused than before. Because he'd never considered he could lose Angel by his own lack of action. What the hell was he supposed to do now?

Amara woke up in the cold bed, alone and distinctly aware that something was wrong. But she was a problem solver, and she would deal with this situation no differently than any other challenge.

She twisted in the sheets, her body still tender from the way Lennox had made love to her until she was a mess of limp limbs. When she'd recovered enough to move, she'd turned around in his arms and found a brief glimpse of reciprocity in his eyes. It wasn't just the physical. It was something stronger that tethered them, making her feel connected to him in a way she hadn't since the night they'd met. And if the fire in his eyes was any indication, he'd felt it, too.

But before she could grab hold of it, it had slipped through her fingers like a silky ribbon, too elusive for her to grasp. Within a second of that iron curtain coming down, he was picking up his clothes and leaving the room. She'd waited for him to come home, thinking they could talk about it, but as midnight crept up, she'd lost her battle with sleep.

After showering and dressing in a red wrap dress that hugged her curves and ensured every eye in the room would be on her, she took one last glimpse in the mirror, running her fingers through her layered waves, so her hair framed her face just right.

She walked down the hall to the nearest guest room and knocked on the door. When she didn't get an answer, she slowly opened it to find Lennox's bed empty and made. Either he made it before he left, or he'd never actually come home.

When she got to the living room, she heard voices coming from the kitchen. She smoothed her hands down her sides and took a breath before she walked through the swinging door that led to the large modern space. Lennox was standing on one side of the counter talking to his campaign manager.

"Morning, Angel." His voice was smooth and light, as if nothing odd had occurred last night. He walked over to her, kissing her lightly on the cheek and leading her back to the counter. "You remember John Christos."

She put on a polite smile and extended her hand to the man. "Good morning, Mr. Christos. It's a bit early for campaign strategizing, isn't it?"

His blue eyes sparkled with mischief, and she realized that if his presence weren't an inconvenience at this moment, she'd probably get along well with this man.

"Sorry, Mrs. Carlisle. Even though Lennox has won the primary, we can't sit back. We've got to keep up with the momentum. I'm glad you're here. It gives me a chance to make sure you're up to speed."

She lifted a brow, smiling over his attempt to finesse

her. "You mean find out if I have any skeletons in my closet that could derail his run."

Again, that sparkle of mischief shone bright in his eyes, causing a chuckle from everyone in the room.

"Lennox, you're in trouble with this one. I don't think you're smart enough to handle her."

"You ain't lying there," Lennox mumbled as he placed a glass of orange juice in front of her.

She ignored Lennox's quip and addressed John. "I don't have a lot of time to break down my background. My family is one of the oldest and wealthiest families in Brooklyn. We're in the business of making money, but we don't make a habit of doing shady business."

She took a sip of the juice before she continued. "I've spent most of my adult life helping my family enlarge its fortune. There hasn't been a lot of time for me to get involved with anything that could be considered scandalous."

"And what about this latest project your company is working on with Falcon Development?"

"When Lennox and I realized who was on the other side of our respective titles, we set up a third-party panel to consider Devereaux Inc.'s application for the permits. My rep tells me we have a few days before we have to submit our final proposal, and then we'll have a final decision. Whatever they decide, both Devereaux Inc. and the city have agreed to abide by."

John scribbled a few things on a notepad before lifting his gaze back to hers.

"Good. Sounds like everything is on the up-and-up. Hopefully there won't be any surprises. If anything does come up, please don't hesitate to let me know. Getting ahead of a scandal is always the key."

She nodded and gave him a cordial smile. "Understood."

She turned away from John and leveled her gaze at Lennox. He stood next to her, but other than the brief kiss he'd placed on her cheek when she entered the kitchen, he hadn't made any physical contact with her yet. She figured it was because they had company. But part of her couldn't shake the feeling he was still avoiding her.

Her plans to clear the air with her husband were ash with John sitting in the middle of the kitchen. Nevertheless, they still needed to talk.

"Hey, do you think we can meet up for lunch today? I need to run something past you."

"We can talk now."

She glanced briefly in John's direction before meeting Lennox's eyes again. "Can't. I'm going to stop in to see Uncle Ace before I head out to run some errands today. With everything that's been going on, I haven't had the chance to spend any quality time with him. I also have a final dress fitting for my bridesmaid's dress for Trey and Jeremiah's wedding."

Lennox nodded. "Okay, where do you want to meet up?"

"Could you pick me up from Trey's apartment? That's where the tailors and seamstresses are meeting the bridal party."

"Sure." He leaned in, giving her a respectful peck on her lips. "I'll see you this afternoon."

She nodded her farewell to John before making her

way through the kitchen door, grabbing her bag and keys from the coatrack in the foyer and leaving the apartment. Hopefully, when she returned, things would be much more settled between her and her husband. Otherwise, she wasn't so sure how they were going to be able to keep their promises to each other. Not if they didn't deal with whatever this was now.

Lennox watched as his wife disappeared behind the swinging kitchen door. As his gaze lingered on her retreating form, he had to force his body not to react. It was an amazing feat considering the way the stretchy material of her dress cradled her lush body.

"That takes one worry off my list."

Lennox pulled his gaze away from the door and looked at John. "What?"

"When you told me you'd married the woman who was carrying your child, I worried that you were rushing into a loveless marriage to salvage your career. Those kinds of setups almost always backfire, and it would've led to an even worse situation for me to have to clean up."

Lennox watched John carefully, trying hard not to give too much away. "And after meeting my wife you're no longer worried about that?"

"Nope, not after seeing the way the two of you were looking at each other. You two are going to burn the camera up on this last leg of the campaign. Even if you weren't leading the polls by fourteen points, the sight of you two together would convince people to vote for you. We need to figure out how we can strategically use this to our advantage. Let's just hope whatever Amara has to say to you doesn't derail all the plans germinating in my head."

Lennox leaned on the counter to try to help him hold his temper. "Again, what the hell are you talking about?"

John stared blankly at him, blinking slowly as if he were trying to process Lennox's words.

"As taken as your new bride is with you, no good has ever come from the phrase 'we need to talk.' Whatever it is, I have the feeling she only spared you because I was here. Did you hog all the covers last night?"

Lennox wished it were that simple. That would mean he'd actually slept with his wife last night.

"You're reading way too much into this. There's nothing wrong."

John lifted both eyebrows. "You're sure? Because it didn't seem that way to me."

Lennox swallowed as his mind replayed the exchange with his wife. Of course, he knew what she wanted to talk about. He'd all but run out on her last night after spending most of the day buried inside her. Suddenly, he could hear Carter's warning from last night ringing in his head. Had she already decided to toss him away?

Refusing to give in to the panic, he took another swig of the juice Angel had left and met John's skeptical gaze.

"My marriage is fine. You have absolutely nothing to worry about."

Lennox just hoped he was right.

# Nineteen

"Stunning."

Amara turned to Trey, who was sitting on the large bed in the center of the room. Due to the estrangement of Trey's father and grandfather, she hadn't grown up in the fold with Stephan, Lyric, Amara, and Ace's ward, Jeremiah. But once she'd blown back onto the scene like a mighty wind, she'd quickly carved out a unique place for herself among the Devereaux cousins.

"You like it?" Trey's question lingered in the air.

Amara returned her gaze to the full-length mirror, admiring the way the champagne one-shouldered gown hung on her curves. She wasn't exactly showing yet, but her pants were beginning to feel a little snug. She'd worried the dress wouldn't fit. But she was pleased with the way the fabric clung to her skin, creating a lovely silhouette.

"I do. You made a great selection, Trey."

Trey stood from the bed and came to Amara's side. "I don't think that glow you have going on has anything to do with my bridesmaid's dress selection. Pregnancy and marriage seem to be agreeing with you."

"The pregnancy is. But the marriage part is up for debate."

When Amara refused to meet Trey's gaze in the mirror, her cousin tugged at her shoulder, bidding her to turn around and face her.

"What's that supposed to mean?"

Amara hesitated to speak the truth of her marriage to anyone. When you came from a family where failure wasn't an option, it wasn't always easy to admit when things were going wrong in your world. But the soft concern she heard in Trey's voice made Amara want to lay all her troubles bare. Maybe because Trey wasn't as entrenched in Devereaux culture yet it felt easier to share. Whatever it was, Amara took her hand and led Trey back to the bed she'd previously sat on.

"Everyone knows my marriage and this baby were a bit of a surprise to Lennox and me. We didn't plan on any of this. But that didn't stop it from feeling right."

Trey leaned in, giving Amara her complete attention. "Are you saying you regret your decision to marry?"

Amara shook her head, then nodded. She didn't know the answer after last night.

She recounted the events that had transpired, as her cousin sat there quietly taking in each new detail.

"I'm really sorry you're going through that," she said when Amara finished. "Have you talked to him about it? It could just be as simple as adjusting to his new role of husband and expectant father. I don't think you have anything else to worry about with him."

"What makes you say that? The man literally left me in bed the minute things seemed like they were becoming more than just physical."

Trey gave Amara's hand a gentle pat as she spoke. "I watched him when you two announced your marriage at Devereaux Manor. Except for when you left to help your mom with the cake, he never left your side, and he kept a protective hand on you almost the entire time. When you left the room, he didn't stop watching the entryway. Those aren't the behaviors of a man that doesn't care about his pregnant wife."

"If he cares so much, why'd he leave when we seemed to be getting closer?"

"Intimacy is scary."

Trey's response rang true in Amara's heart. Fear of loving Lennox had plagued her and caused her to withdraw into herself, too.

"Talk to him, Amara. I'm sure whatever it is, once you two have a chance to hammer it out, things will get right back to normal."

"For someone who just found her way into this family, you sure do give great cousin advice."

Trey leaned in, touching her cheek to Amara's and squeezing her in a sideways hug.

"I'm great at everything I do."

Amara chuckled and reveled in the comfort of her cousin's embrace.

"If I couldn't tell by looking at you, that famous Devereaux confidence leaves no doubt you're one of us. I'm really glad you're my cousin. Thank you for the advice, and for letting me take part in your special day."

Trey gave her one more squeeze before she pulled back, sharing a broad smile with Amara. "I'm glad you're my cousin, too."

"Amara! Get out here now!"

Both Amara and Trey stood quickly when they heard Stephan calling them into the living room. Without changing back into her street clothes, Amara was the first to make it down the hall, finding Jeremiah, his best friend Josiah, Lyric and Stephan standing in the middle of the living room.

"What happened?"

Stephan moved to her side and pointed to the television where Abby Phillip sat behind the CNN anchor desk with a breaking-news runner ticking across the bottom of the screen.

"This just in. Documents have surfaced suggesting a backdoor deal signed off on by New York City mayoral hopeful Lennox Carlisle with his new wife's company, Devereaux Incorporated, in what some would call a serious mismanagement of his current office. The project is expected to displace longtime residents, in direct conflict with the candidate's campaign pledge to increase the availability of affordable housing."

Amara's jaw dropped as she watched photos of her initial proposal for the permits fill the television screen.

"Please tell me those are fakes," Trey said in a clipped tone.

"Those documents are from the first proposal Devereaux Inc. put together, before Lennox and I knew we'd be working together. After we recused ourselves from the process, the terms of the deal would have changed to limit the impact on the neighborhood and prevent further gentrification."

"Did you accidentally send the originals to the third-party panel? Have they been considering the wrong deal all this time?"

Amara tried to pull her chaotic thoughts together long enough to scan her memory for anything that could reasonably explain this situation.

"Trey, that couldn't have happened. My team reworked that proposal from scratch to make it more favorable for the city, to get them to agree to our terms more readily. Lennox did not have any say over the new proposal. The only people to see the original proposal were the members of my team, and Lennox, when I handed them to him at our first meeting in his office. And before you even ask it, there's no way he'd do something like this. It's significantly more damaging to him than us."

"How did this get out, Amara?" Jeremiah asked. As co-CEO of the company, he certainly had a right to an answer. But as the report kept alluding to some sort of collusion, she couldn't focus on what Jeremiah was saying.

"Amara, did you hear me?"

"I heard you, Jeremiah," she answered with a sharp glint of annoyance in her voice. "I don't know, and I can't stand here trying to figure it out right now. I gotta get to Lennox."

She turned down the hall, taking the bridesmaid's dress off quickly as she went, praying she didn't rip it to shreds as she tried to get out of it. When she was finally changed, she grabbed her purse and headed downstairs. She was in the process of calling a car to pick her up when the blacked-out SUV Lennox used for official travel pulled up to the curb.

Lennox's driver exited the SUV and turned to face her. "Mrs. Carlisle, the councilman sent me for you."

He opened the back door for her and she got into the vehicle. Once she was settled and her seat belt was secured, the driver slowly pulled into traffic.

As she combed through her mind to try to figure out how those documents were leaked, her phone vibrated in her purse.

Her stomach sank when she saw her great-aunt Martha's name flashing across the screen. It could not be a coincidence that she was receiving a call from the woman now.

"Aunt Martha, now isn't such a great time. I'll have to call you back later."

"What's wrong, niece?" the woman crooned a little too sweetly over the phone. When Amara didn't answer, the woman cackled like a cartoon villain before she continued. "Let me ask you this. How does it feel to watch your dreams blow up in your face? Can you accept that everything you've ever wanted has been cruelly snatched away?"

Amara felt rage welling up in her chest. She took a silent breath, pressing her anger down until she was certain she could speak without her voice cracking.

"I don't know how you did this," she began, "but I promise you, if this negatively impacts my husband's career, I will end you."

"Niece, how I did this is unimportant. Just know I

still have friends in high places, and I know exactly where to dig to find out the dirt the Devereauxs are trying to hide."

Amara closed her fist so tight she could feel the bite of her nails in her palm. Even as the black sheep of the family, Martha still wielded more influence than most. That was especially evident considering the mess she'd managed to stir up.

"We're family, Martha. Why would you seek to destroy me? Why would you try to compromise the company, your family's legacy, with such a decisive blow?"

Martha laughed again, the shrill sound spilling like ice down Amara's spine. "It's called efficiency, dear. I just killed two birds with one stone. The Devereaux family turned against me, and I won't stop until I've paid every single one of you back."

Amara spoke through clenched teeth. "Be careful, Auntie. This is a war you don't want. There's nowhere you can hide. I'm coming for you."

"Bring. It. On." The line went dead after Martha spoke those three words.

Amara was too heated about what Martha had done to be insulted by the fact that the woman had hung up on her. As she returned her phone to her purse, the driver pulled over and parked in front of Lennox's office.

When she stepped into Lennox's office, she took a cursory look around. The room was full of people she marginally recognized from Lennox's house the night of the primary. They were all hovering around her husband as he sat holding his head in his hands.

Her protective instincts were already on full alert

after speaking to her great-aunt. Seeing him look so helpless there made her want to lash out at the world.

She slammed the door behind her, getting the room's attention. "Everyone out now." Her tone must have conveyed she wasn't in the mood for nonsense today, because they all scurried out, including John, the campaign manager.

Finally alone with her husband, she walked toward Lennox, placing a hand on his shoulder for comfort. He quickly grabbed it before looking up at her.

"Angel." His voice was rough, filled with more despair than anger. "I don't want to ask you this, but I have to. Please tell me you didn't do this."

She flinched as if he'd struck her. The truth was, he may as well have. The question was like taking a sledgehammer to glass, breaking her heart and turning it into tiny shards of glass in one decisive blow.

"I don't want to believe you had anything to do with this. But my team traced the emails that contained the leaked files. They came from your address."

She was hurt, because her first thought had been to run here and protect him while his first thought was to believe trumped-up evidence against her. It stung more than she could bear.

For all her doubts about their relationship, she was still holding on to the hope that they could make this work. But when she saw the expectant look in his eyes as he waited for her response, she understood that Lennox would always prioritize their child and business over her feelings. And after their child was born, she didn't think Lennox would have even the slightest bit of love left over for her.

If she couldn't have her husband's love, his trust, she would at least walk away with her dignity. She pulled her hand away from his, slowly letting it drop to her side as she stiffened her shoulders.

"If you need me to confirm that, then you don't know me as well as you should."

He stood, remorse filling his expression for a brief second, but it was too late. The damage had already been done. He didn't believe in her, and from the looks of it, he never would.

"I'll admit I messed up in sleeping with you without telling you who I was. But I haven't lied to you once since we've been together. I've done everything you've asked of me to make this situation right, including legally binding myself to a man who will never love me, even when I knew I was falling in love with him."

Lennox was silent for a moment, seemingly processing what she'd said. But in true Lennox fashion, when he finally spoke, he ignored matters of her heart and stuck to the business at hand. "Angel, you can't expect me to ignore this breach. That information came from somewhere. I sure as hell wouldn't gain from it being exposed. It would be irresponsible of me to pretend the possibility doesn't exist that you leaked this."

"Well," she continued, "I should've seen that coming. That's all you've ever seen me as, some flighty, irresponsible woman who would sabotage everything she's ever worked for to get what she wants in the moment. I had one lapse in judgment in sleeping with you and not telling you who I was. For you, that somehow equates to me trying to destroy your career?"

"I didn't say that, Angel." He squeezed her hand

again, as if it would somehow diffuse her anger. Little did he know, she wasn't the slightest bit angry, just hurt.

"You know what? I'm done being your sacrificial lamb. I'll remain married to you for however long you need me to. After all, that was the agreement I made. But from this moment on, the only thing you and I will share is our child. If you need me, I'll be back home in Clinton Hill where I belong."

Without another word, she stepped away from his desk and walked straight to the door. With each step, it felt like a sharp, serrated knife was plunged into her chest, ripping at her insides. But no matter how much she wanted to crumble, she wouldn't give him the satisfaction of seeing her broken.

Not now, not ever.

# Twenty

"Hey, you doing okay?"

Amara shifted in her chair, trying to force the muscles of her face into a friendly smile. She'd been doing that all day as she helped Trey get ready for the wedding, posed for bridal party pictures, and stood at the altar with the bride and groom as they exchanged vows.

But now, as Stephan stood in front of her at the reception, asking about her well-being, she couldn't muster enough strength to put a smile on her face and put Stephan's obvious concern to rest.

She picked up her glass of apple cider in a mock toast, tipping it toward him. "Of course, I am."

He pulled an empty chair from the table and positioned it in front of hers. Leaning in, he took her hand, trying his best to convey the concern written all over his face.

"Don't pity me. This is all my fault."

"How do you figure that?"

She took a deep breath, trying her best to offload the weight of all she'd been concealing over the course of her relationship with Lennox.

"Lennox certainly thinks so."

"Did he accuse you of doing this?"

She shook her head, recalling the conversation she'd had with Lennox. "Not technically. But he did ask me to confirm I hadn't done it."

"That couldn't have felt good."

"It didn't," she admitted. "Although, after everything I've done to him, I can't really blame him."

Stephan tilted his head and scanned her face for clues to her meaning.

Too tired to hide her transgressions, she succinctly recounted the summarized version of how she ended up pregnant by and married to Lennox Carlisle.

"Cousin." Stephan spoke cautiously as he digested all she'd shared.

"I know, Stephan."

He dropped his head, shaking it.

"How did Lennox take it when he found out who you are?"

She laughed heartily. "He was pissed and demanded I marry him, or he'd go to Grandfather and tell him what I'd done and refuse to even consider Devereaux Inc.'s permit application."

Stephan sat back in his chair, blowing out an exhausted huff as he watched her.

"Amara, I'd love to go all protective cousin for you and snatch Lennox by his collar. But what you did, the situation you put him in, I can't say that I blame him for the way he reacted. What were you thinking?"

"I wasn't," she admitted. Why lie? Everything had disintegrated into dust, there was no use protecting the illusion now. "But surprisingly, that wouldn't be the last stupid thing I did."

He pinched the bridge of his nose before settling a knowing gaze on her. "You fell in love with your fake husband, didn't you?"

"And now, for the second time in as many months, his affiliation to me is screwing up his professional life. He could lose everything he's worked so hard for because Martha wanted to prove a point to me."

She could see the muscle at his jaw tighten at the mention of his mother's name.

"You have a lot to answer for where Lennox is concerned. But my mother's vindictive streak isn't one of them. Have you determined how she was able to make this happen?"

"She found someone in our IT department to exploit, a man who was desperate for the money to pay for medical treatment for his sick daughter. The truth is, after finding out why he did it, I couldn't really be mad with him. I fired him, of course. But I also contacted the hospital and made myself the guarantor for her medical bills. That baby shouldn't suffer simply because her father had the misfortune of falling into Martha's clutches."

Her cousin reached for her hand and this time, she held on tightly, needing his strength more than she ever had in the past.

"This isn't your fault, Amara. The fault lies with my mother. She did this. Not you."

"It doesn't matter," she answered as she struggled to keep the pain out of her voice. "I risked Lennox's job for selfish reasons, and then my family banged the nail into his professional coffin. He could be impeached for this, Stephan."

"No one ever said loving a Devereaux would be easy, Cousin."

She lifted a brow, wondering how many celebratory cocktails her cousin had downed before joining her.

"You mean 'loathing.' Love has never lived in this relationship."

"Sometimes it's hard to see the truth of things when you're too close to them. Trust me, distance can bring great clarity."

She could see the shadows of his demons flitting across his eyes and knew her cousin was speaking from experience.

"Amara, I watched him watching you the night you brought him to meet the family. That man is sprung and possessive. This might not have started out as a love match, but the way that man was looking at you, there's more than convenience and duty binding him to you."

Her heart fluttered. She wanted to grab hold of the picture he was painting, but doubt wouldn't let her.

"Trey said the same thing. I wish you both were right, Steph…"

He held up his hand. "Just stop, Amara. Stop and listen to me. If I were you, I'd shut down this personal pity party and get my shit together so I could fight for

my man. Because if I had a man looking at me the way
Lennox looks at you, I'd go to any length to keep him."

"I don't know how to keep him." She struggled to
keep her tears at bay but lost the battle. "Even before
this happened, things weren't great. He treated me well.
But he was always adamant love would never be part
of the equation."

"Listen." Stephan leaned in and wiped her tears with
a gentle thumb. "As a gay man, I have a unique perspective. Being a man and loving men, I can tell you
something you might not know. Men are stupid and we
have no idea what we want or need."

She narrowed her gaze at him and then slipped into
a fit of giggles that led to more tears.

"You're a mess. You know that, right?" she finally
said as she got ahold of herself.

"Yeah, but you still love me, though. So listen to
me. If you love Lennox, you've gotta make this right
for him. You're a Devereaux, and with the exception of
my mean-ass mama, we protect our own. You've just
got to ask yourself if you love Lennox enough to consider him one of us."

She loved Lennox, there was no question about it.
But had he ever truly been hers? Did he belong to her
and by extension to the Devereauxs?

Then she remembered something her uncle Ace mentioned when he brought Jeremiah, a kid off the street, to
live with him at sixteen. He'd told everyone Jeremiah
was family. And when she asked how, he answered,
"By love." He was right. Loving Lennox was the only
qualifier she needed to claim him as one of her own.
And Devereauxs never had, never would abandon one

of their people. And she decided in that moment, she wouldn't start now.

Satisfied, he'd gotten through to her, he gifted her with a knowing smile. "Glad you're seeing things my way. Now, let me go get Lyric to help you fix your makeup, because you are looking a hot mess right now."

"You know you're sounding like you share your mama's mean gene, right?"

"That's a low blow, but you ain't wrong. At least I use my powers for good, though."

"A fact I will forever be grateful for." She stood up and pointed at him. "Go ahead and get Lyric so she can hurry up and fix my face. I feel like there's a Cupid Shuffle with my name on it waiting for me on the dance floor."

# Twenty-One

"Len, this can't go on."

Lennox sat at his desk, staring out a nearby window at nothing in particular as his campaign manager continued his diatribe.

"If you don't address these allegations, this could end up turning into an official investigation for collusion."

Lennox hung his head in defeat. "There was no collusion. You know that. Any investigation will show that I went above and beyond what's required to avoid any conflict of interest."

John stopped pacing in the middle of his room, dropping in the chair on the opposite side of Lennox's desk.

"You're right. But by the time you're absolved, you'll have already lost the election. You've already dropped three points in the polls. We have to do something now before it's too late."

John was right, of course. He needed to act. But since his Angel had gone, he couldn't seem to focus on anything but his pain.

He chuckled at the irony of it all. He'd fought so hard to avoid this pain, doing everything in his power to keep his distance so he wouldn't fall in love with her. And yet he'd still managed to let things deteriorate so badly that he'd pushed himself right into despair.

"John, I know you're right. But my mind isn't on this right now. Angel moved out and she won't talk to me so we can work this out."

John's face bore compassion, which only made Lennox feel worse.

"Lennox, you can't ignore this anymore." John handed him a printed piece of paper. Lennox scanned through it to see a very truthful, yet cautious public statement.

John watched Lennox carefully as he spoke. "The press is already gathered in the lobby. All you have to do is go downstairs and read it."

He huffed, waving the statement in the air. "Let's get this over with."

Lennox stood at the podium in the lobby, looking out into the sea of cameras and reporters. Before he could even speak, they were hurling questions at him, each feeling like a body shot thrown by a champion fighter.

"Please, hold your questions until the end," Lennox said calmly, using every trick he knew to keep himself still and focused. "A lot has been said in the last week and I'm here to set the record straight. There was no collusion. Everything about the application process Devereaux Inc. underwent was aboveboard."

He took a breath and before he could speak again, a reporter interrupted. "Councilman, if there was no collusion, can you explain the details of the emails leaked to the public?"

"He can't." The room went silent as a familiar voice boomed from one side of the atrium, hitting Lennox square in the chest. "But I will."

He scanned the space, and saw his wife moving through the crowd, making her way to the podium. When she got to him, he covered the microphone with his hand and leaned closer to her ear. "What are you doing here, Angel?"

"Saving your ass. The question is, will you let me?"

They held each other's gaze much longer than professionalism allowed. But to hell with professionalism. His wife was here, and all he wanted to do was cherish this moment, no matter if it was playing out in front of the cameras.

He stepped aside, and she took her place in front of the microphone. Suddenly, he saw all the things that had drawn him to her on that very first night. She was strong, self-assured. And by the way she turned slightly and gave him a sexy wink, whatever it was she had planned, he knew she'd end up owning the room.

"Good morning, everyone. As I was saying, Councilman Carlisle can't give you the details of the proposal. What was released was an initial deal memo we used in-house as a springboard for any negotiations Devereaux Inc. engages in.

"Devereaux Inc. is a for-profit company. As such,

it's always our desire to make the best deal possible for the business. But this deal memo was a draft. It was never signed by me or anyone at the company. As many of you may know, the councilman and I recently married. Our relationship began prior to Devereaux Inc. filing the permit applications. While I had previously worked on the Falcon deal, at the time of our wedding, I wasn't assigned to it. But then I became lead counsel of Devereaux Inc. due to a family emergency. We saw the potential for conflict of interest and took immediate steps. The city set up a third-party panel to evaluate the permits and both the councilman and I recused ourselves from the negotiations to avoid any impropriety. But I'm here today to set the record straight and make Devereaux Inc.'s position clear."

She raised her head to glance out at the audience. Once she captured their attention, she continued.

"Devereaux Inc. was the victim of a targeted internal breach. My email was compromised by an employee who has since been terminated. Neither the councilman nor his office had any involvement in this."

Angel acknowledged one of the many reporters who were frantically waving their hands in the audience.

"Mrs. Carlisle. You're married to the councilman. Why should the public believe you?"

"That's simple," Angel answered, as smooth and calm as ever. "Because it's the truth. And if that's not enough, I have a signed affidavit from the third-party panel established to process and rule on the permits."

"So if this deal memo was just a draft and never submitted for formal consideration, what are the actual terms of the application submitted?"

Angel continued, unfazed. "I'm glad you asked that question. I have a signed affidavit from my second-in-command, Sergio Dennison, stipulating that after further study, he and his team amended their proposal to make sure Devereaux Inc. was providing the most benefit for both the business and the neighborhood slated for construction.

"On behalf of Devereaux inc. Mr. Dennison has committed to investing in the existing small businesses in the area and making sure residents aren't pushed out by this development. He further proposes that Devereaux Inc. reserve fifty percent of the project's rental units for lower-income families. An elaborate park and garden area for families and seniors to enjoy a bit of nature will be created. And finally, he's included plans for two brand new community centers and funding for their maintenance and programming. The panel's affidavit includes the full proposal, so the details can be found there."

Because he'd recused himself from the process, Lennox hadn't previously known about the new deal terms. As Amara listed them all, he had to lock his knees to keep himself from dropping where he stood.

She had heard him, heard everything he'd said about urban renewal.

"Devereaux Inc. is dedicated to helping better our community in line with the councilman's vision," she continued. "We think we've finally come to a solution that will bring much-needed dollars and employment to this part of Brooklyn without discarding the people who have built it from the ground up. Thank you for your time."

Angel relinquished the podium to him, giving him a gracious smile as she stepped aside. Wanting to talk to her, but knowing he had a job to do, he gave her arm a squeeze, hoping it conveyed his gratitude.

He returned to the podium, finishing things up as quickly as he could. In his mind, her willingness to help him had to mean she was ready to address their problems. He wouldn't allow himself to believe anything else. And when he realized Angel had somehow disappeared, he wasn't deterred. He wanted his wife back, and now he knew he finally had a chance.

# Twenty-Two

Amara rushed toward her office door ignoring her assistant, who was trying to get her attention. "Whatever it is can wait. I just need a moment."

Two steps inside her office, and she knew what her assistant was trying to tell her. Her grandfather was sitting on her couch with one leg crossed over the other, making him look like the stately gentleman he was.

Too exhausted from the emotional upheaval of seeing her husband for the first time since the permit story broke, she didn't have the energy to listen to him recount all the ways she'd messed things up.

"I've had a long day, Grandfather. So if you're here to tell me how I've gone too far once again, I'm really not up for it. This deal might not be as lucrative as the original proposal, but it was the right thing to do for the community. And I'm going to make sure Devereaux Inc. fulfills every promise."

He remained silent for a long moment, until the tension in the room reached the breaking point.

"I agree with you," he finally said. "This was the right deal to make."

She went to the couch and sat down. Trying to figure out the angle he was working, she crossed her arms and gave him a skeptical look.

"You agree with me?"

"I do," he replied easily, nodding. "You've been driven by monetary success for so long, I was afraid you'd eventually end up destroyed by your greed. But the proposal you spoke about today, that took heart and confidence. Two things you must have equally in order to be both successful and responsible. This was the lawyer I was trying to mold you into being. I'm so proud of you."

Confusion welled up inside her. She'd waited so long to hear him speak those words to her, and now that he was, her brain was having a hard time wrapping itself around what was unfolding right before her very eyes.

"You're proud of me? After all this time? But this wasn't even my deal. Sergio and his team put this together."

His relaxed posture stiffened as he watched her, as if something she'd said struck a nerve.

"That may be technically true," her grandfather responded. "But you were the leader that gave him and his team the space to work and you listened to their recommendation. So yeah, I'm proud of you. All that took courage."

She must have remained silent too long because he asked, "Why is it such a surprise that I'm proud of you?"

"Because you've spent every day of our working relationship telling me how I don't compare to my mother as a lawyer."

The light in his brown eyes dimmed as he processed what she was saying to him.

"Is that what you believed? That I didn't think you measured up?"

"Yes."

She went to stand, attempting to put a bit of distance between them. But he laid his warm hand atop hers as sadness filled his gaze.

"Amara, if that's how I made you feel, I'm terribly sorry. It was never my intention to make you believe you were lacking in any way. I simply thought I was giving you something to aspire to. I didn't realize I was causing you pain."

The sincerity in his voice made her breath hitch, and the tears began to fall. And just like when she was a little girl who cried when she'd fallen off her bike onto the unforgiving concrete, he pulled her into his arms and rocked her back and forth.

"You are the best of us, Amara. That's why I've always been so hard on you. Not because I lacked faith. But because I was nearly blinded by the brilliance of your potential. All I can ask is that you forgive an old fool for pushing you away when all I wanted to do was nurture your innate talent. Please forgive me."

Of course, she wanted to. Accepting his apology meant she could finally allow herself to believe he had faith in her.

She pulled back, and he must have seen the doubt in her eyes, because he gifted her with a gracious smile before speaking again.

"Amara, what have I always told you?"

"Words are meaningless unless they're in a contract or backed up by action." He'd drilled that into her over and over again. His motto had been the foundation for so many of the contract negotiations she'd won for Devereaux Inc. Which was why Lennox's accusation cut so deep. It was proof he really didn't know her. And if he didn't know her, there was no chance he could possibly love her.

"Exactly," her grandfather replied with a wobbly smile. "So let me get on with why I came here today. You've proven yourself ready for the job and all the things that come with it, both good and bad. I turned in my retirement forms today. As soon as they're finalized, I will name you as my permanent successor. The person most qualified to take on the job."

If she hadn't been sitting, she might have fallen over. Hell, she still might. This moment was the culmination of everything she'd ever wanted. And even as happiness filled her, there was still an echo of darkness surrounding her heart because she couldn't share this with the man she loved.

When her grandfather left, Amara stood at the window of her office in Clinton Hill, trying to make sense of all that had happened today. She'd done something good for her community and her business, pulled Lennox back from the professional brink and won the promotion she'd worked so hard for. She should be pleased with herself. Instead, her mind kept focusing on the one thing she'd managed to lose in all of this: her husband.

Before she could sink further into despair, she was distracted by a knock on her door.

"Come in," she answered without turning away from the window. She didn't need her visitor to see her misery, which she didn't have enough energy to cover up at the moment.

"Angel."

The rich tone of Lennox's voice sent a tremor through her body. Slightly afraid she'd managed to conjure him up, she turned around to find him standing near her desk.

He was still wearing the navy Brooks Brothers suit from the press conference. But his tie was gone and the first button of his collar was unbuttoned. Whatever this visit was about, it wasn't business. He'd never negotiate without his full corporate armor in place.

"Please forgive me for just popping up. Your secretary told me I could come in. I guess you haven't announced that you left me?"

"I told you, I'll keep up the pretenses of our marriage in public for as long as you need me to. I just can't live with a man who has so little faith in me."

She saw something akin to regret flitter in his eyes.

"Not to be rude, Lennox. But what are you doing here?"

He chuckled as a sad smile crept onto his face. "I'm here for a couple of reasons. The first, how did you get Falcon to agree to everything you promised at the press conference today? They're taking on extra building I'm sure wasn't part of the initial deal."

"Devereaux Inc. will cover the cost of building the additional structures. Because the terms I negotiated between Falcon and Devereaux Inc. are so favorable, we still stand to make a healthy profit from the deal. We can afford the added expense."

"And the powers that be at Devereaux Inc. are okay with this?"

"Exceedingly so," she answered. "My grandfather's actually naming me as his permanent successor. I got the job I've always wanted." She narrowed her gaze and scanned his face. Something was off and his questions, though seemingly benign, made the lawyer in her suspicious.

"What's all this about, Lennox? If you're here because you're worrying that this will somehow backfire on you, don't. The city will get everything I promised on behalf of Devereaux Inc. You didn't have to come all the way down here for that."

He stepped closer to her, until she could smell his sweet and spicy cologne, drawing her into his powerful orbit.

"No, that's not why I'm here. According to John, I've recovered from my drop in the polls. I'm still in the lead to win this thing. John says it's because you're a miracle worker. I'm sure if you ever got tired of working for Devereaux Inc., he'd definitely take you on his team."

"He couldn't afford me." She tilted her head as she waited for him to get to the point.

"I came down here because I wanted...needed to see my wife."

When she remained silent, he closed his eyes for a brief second, before returning his amber gaze to her.

"I was wrong, Angel."

"About accusing me of sabotaging you? Yes, you were."

"Yes, I was wrong for that. But I was wrong for so much more. Namely, keeping you at arm's length when all I wanted to do was pull you closer."

He cupped her cheek in his warm palm, the mere touch causing her to involuntarily moan.

"I'm sorry that I was so afraid of being hurt by you, I refused to give in to what I could see so clearly."

His words, coupled with the warmth of his touch, were like an elixir for every pain she'd experienced during their marriage. But she couldn't help worrying about whether this was just temporary relief that only masked the symptoms or an actual cure that would revive her wounded heart.

"Why are you saying this to me? I don't understand, Lennox. From the moment you found out I was pregnant, you've offered me everything except your heart. You clearly stated love wasn't on the table and I stupidly went along with it even though I knew I was falling in love with you. What's changed now? Because I can't go back to loving someone who will only run from me the closer I try to get to him. I won't condemn myself to a life of having to put myself back together every time you reject me. So, tell me, what is it you intend to gain from this visit?"

His usually stoic expression cracked and his mask slipped just the tiniest bit, the same way it had the day of her sonogram.

"I came to beg my wife's forgiveness for treating her so terribly and being careless with her heart. I came to tell you I'm done with letting fear rule me, and if you'll have me, I'll spend the rest of my life worshipping you. I came to say that I love you, and although that scares the hell out of me, the idea of losing you is a fate worse than death. I came to beg you to take me back even though I know I don't deserve you."

Hot tears welled up in her eyes, scorching her skin as they slid down her face. Could this day really grant her all the things she wanted at once?

"I want to believe you, Lennox. But I'm afraid. This entire marriage has been about your career and our baby. And as much as I know you already love this child, I want you to love me for me, and not because you see me as some human vessel for your baby."

He slid his gaze over her face before he responded. "I am a fool for ever letting you believe the only thing I wanted from you was this baby. It's you, Angel. It's always been you."

He leaned down, letting his lips finally touch hers. It was the most satisfying thing she'd felt in a long while, but it also stoked a fiery need that seemed to consume her right where she stood.

He broke their kiss, leaving them both struggling to catch their breath. "It's why I was so adamant about fidelity and you wearing my rings. I needed the world to know you were mine because the thought of you turning to anyone else made me want to commit violence."

He pulled her back to him, searing her with a second kiss that left her desperate for more when he tore his mouth from hers. "Please, baby," he pleaded. "Tell me you love me."

She should've made him suffer more. She should've

taken the upper hand and cast him aside. It was nothing less than what he deserved. But slowly, she recognized that she needed to focus on what *she* deserved. She deserved the elation of being loved by this man. She deserved the joy of being showered with his love. And once she'd come to the conclusion that what she deserved was happiness and that he was her happiness, her choice became clear.

"I do love you, Lennox."

"Tell me you'll come back to me. That you'll be mine."

"I'll come back," she answered, before initiating a kiss of her own. "I'll be yours." She let her kisses travel to the sharp angle of his jaw and downward until she reached the curve of his neck. "Now, I've got a condition for you."

He wrapped his arms tighter around her, letting her know he'd heard her, even though he didn't verbally respond.

"I need you to go lock my office door so you can come back here and show me just how much you've missed me since I've been gone."

He pulled far enough away from her to look down into her eyes, gifting her with his mischievous smile.

"Just one more reason why I love you so much, Angel."

"Why's that?"

"Because you, my brilliant, beautiful wife, are really good at anticipating what I want even before I recognize what it is."

She wrapped her arms around his neck and nodded. "You're right, Councilman, I do know how to give you what you want. Now hurry up and lock the door so you can give me what I need."

His expression was filled with happiness as he rushed to the door. And for the first time, she realized she didn't feel the need to protect her heart from him. From this moment on, she would never have to hide the love that was bursting through the seams of her soul.

When he returned to her, she pulled him down into a fiery kiss. "You ready to show me just how much you love me today, Councilman Carlisle?"

"Yes, ma'am. Today and every day to come for the rest of our lives."

\* \* \* \* \*

*Don't miss a single*
*Devereaux Inc. novel*
*by LaQuette!*

A Very Intimate Takeover
Backstage Benefits
One Night Expectations

*Available exclusively*
*from Harlequin Desire.*

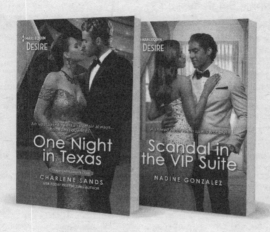

## #2875 BOYFRIEND LESSONS

*Texas Cattleman's Club: Ranchers and Rivals*
by Sophia Singh Sasson

Ready to break out of her shell, shy heiress Caitlyn Lattimore needs the help of handsome businessman Dev Mallik to sharpen her dating skills. Soon, fake dates lead to steamy nights. But can this burgeoning relationship survive their complicated histories?

## #2876 THE SECRET HEIR RETURNS

*Dynasties: DNA Dilemma* • by Joss Wood

Secret heir Sutton Marchant has no desire to connect with his birth family or anyone else. But when he travels to accept his inheritance, he can't ignore his attraction to innkeeper Lowrie Lewis. Can he put the past behind him to secure his future?

## #2877 ROCKY MOUNTAIN RIVALS

*Return to Catamount* • by Joanne Rock

Fleur Barclay, his brother's ex, should be off-limits to successful rancher Drake Alexander, especially since they've always despised one another. But when Fleur arrives back in their hometown, there's a spark neither can ignore, no matter how much they try...

## #2878 A GAME BETWEEN FRIENDS

*Locketts of Tuxedo Park* • by Yahrah St. John

After learning he'll never play again, football star Xavier Lockett finds solace in the arms of singer Porscha Childs, until a misunderstanding tears them apart. When they meet again, the heat is still there. But they might lose each other once more if they can't resolve their mistakes...

## #2879 MILLION-DOLLAR CONSEQUENCES

*The Dunn Brothers* • by Jessica Lemmon

Actor Isaac Dunn needs a date to avoid scandal, and his agent's sister, Meghan Squire, is perfect. But pretending leads to one real night... and a baby on the way. Will this convenient arrangement withstand the consequences—and the sparks—between them?

## #2880 CORNER OFFICE CONFESSIONS

*The Kane Heirs* • by Cynthia St. Aubin

To oust his twin brother from the family company, CEO Samuel Kane sets him up to break the company's cardinal rule—no workplace relationships. But it's *Samuel* who finds himself tempted when Arlie Banks awakes a passion that could cost him everything...

*Focused on finishing an upcoming album, sound engineer Teagan Woodson and guitarist Maxton McCoy struggle to keep things professional as their attraction grows. But agreeing to "just a fling" may lead to everything around them falling apart...*

*Read on for a sneak peek at*
After Hours Temptation
*by Kianna Alexander.*

Maxton eyed Teagan and asked, "Isn't there something I didn't get to see?"

She smiled. "If you mean my bedroom, you gotta earn it, playboy."

"Sounds like a challenge," he quipped.

She shook her head. "No. More of a requirement."

He laughed, then gently dragged the tip of his index finger along her jawline. "You're going to make me work for this. I just know it."

Her answer was a sultry smile. "We'll just have to see what happens."

"Truth is, I really don't have the time for a relationship right now."

If she took offense at his statement, she didn't show it. "Neither do I."

"So, what are we doing here?"

She shrugged. "A fling? A dalliance? I don't think it really matters what we call it, so long as we both understand what it is…and what it isn't."

Their gazes met and held, and the sparkle of mischief in her eyes threatened to do him in. "Enlighten me, Teagan. What will we be doing, exactly?"

"We hang out…have a little fun. No strings, no commitments. And, above all, we don't let this thing interfere with our work or our lives." She pressed her open palm against his chest. "That is, if you think you can handle it."

"Seems reasonable." *I like this approach. Seems like we're on one accord.*

Her smile deepened. "Tomorrow is my only other free day for a while. Why don't you meet me at the Creamery, right near Piedmont Park? Say around seven?"

"I'll be there." He wanted to kiss her but couldn't read her thoughts on the matter. So he grazed his fingertip over her soft glossy lips instead.

"See you then," she whispered.

Satisfied, he opened the front door and stepped out into the afternoon sunshine.

*Don't miss what happens next in…*
After Hours Temptation
*by Kianna Alexander.*

*Available June 2022 wherever*
*Harlequin Desire books and ebooks are sold.*

Harlequin.com

# *Love Harlequin romance?*

## DISCOVER.

Be the first to find out about promotions, news and exclusive content!

Facebook.com/HarlequinBooks

Twitter.com/HarlequinBooks

Instagram.com/HarlequinBooks

Pinterest.com/HarlequinBooks

YouTube.com/HarlequinBooks

ReaderService.com

## EXPLORE.

Sign up for the Harlequin e-newsletter and download a free book from any series at **TryHarlequin.com**

## CONNECT.

Join our Harlequin community to share your thoughts and connect with other romance readers!
**Facebook.com/groups/HarlequinConnection**

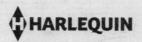